A CAGE OF GOLD AND LIES

Published by Fairies and Fantasy Pty Ltd 2020

A Cage of Gold and Lies copyright © 2020 Selina Fenech

All rights reserved.

www.selinafenech.com

ISBN: 978-1-922390-42-4 (eBook)

ISBN: 978-1-922390-43-1 (paperback)

ISBN: 978-1-922390-44-8 (hardcover)

A CAGE OF GOLD AND LIES

A RUMPELSTILTSKIN RETELLING

SELINA A FENECH

PROLOGUE

WHEN I WAS a child I dared to believe in fairy tales.

Growing up in danger and poverty, it was easy to dream of being plucked from squalor and magically delivered into a better life.

Then I found out that magic was real.

But it had skipped over me, and instead, granted all my wishes to my best friend.

The honks and bellowing of road rage blasted from around the corner, dragging me from the bitter reverie that overtook me every time I walked by the public housing block where Rahanna used to live. Her family was still there—living in the apartment two floors up with the graffiti over the boarded window—but they were planning on moving somewhere nicer soon. I wanted to wish them well. I should feel happy for them.

The sweltering afternoon sun made the city of Oramont swim in a golden, grimy glow. My younger sister's sweaty hand slipped in mine as I walked her home from school, but I was just happy she was letting me hold it. She rarely did these days. She was a big tough nine-year-old now, after all.

"Zari, you think Rahanna married a prince?" Nia asked. She must have seen me staring at the derelict apartments.

"Maybe," I muttered.

Rahanna and I had found each other not long after my family made it to the area, and we had quickly become inseparable. Then one day, about six months back, she'd shown me she could conjure magic.

Real, swirling colors, things-moving-on-their-own *magic*.

The fairy tales my mother read to me as a child crashed into real life and I watched as events played out just like they did in the books. Out of nowhere, Rahanna was offered a high-paying job at a billionaire's estate. They didn't care that she was nineteen and had no legal citizenship status. She was swept off overnight to the delight of her family who received her paychecks back home.

If the extravagant balls, handsome suitors, gowns, castles and a prince to marry came next, I didn't know. It had been months since I'd heard from her. She hadn't even bothered to call. Too rich and fancy for her old friends now.

"I bet he's really gorgeous." My sister looked up at me with big, brown eyes. Her dark hair frayed loose from the braid I'd done that morning, curls clinging to the sweat at her temples. "And she met him at a fancy dinner with a huge swan carved from ice where they drink champagne like this." She pursed her lips and mimed taking a sip from a skinny flute glass with her pinky high in the air, then chortled an upper-crust laugh.

I managed a half smile. It had been fun dreaming about what Rahanna's new life must have been like when she'd first left. Nia and I had giggled late into the nights, roleplaying eating caviar hors d'oeuvres as we swooped around in imaginary ballgowns and coyly fended off the many advances of billionaire members of royalty. It was fun to fantasize about because in the beginning there was some hope that maybe Rahanna would take us with her. At least throw us a few scraps.

I didn't enjoy daydreaming anymore.

Why couldn't it have been me?

"Princes don't exist. Not for people like us." The words snapped from my mouth before I could censor them. Rahanna had taken the chance to make a better life for herself, and I would have done the same in her position. I shouldn't sully her memory with my jealousy. I softened my tone. "But Rahanna is lucky to be working a good job now with enough money to buy anything she and her family need."

Nia made a vomit sound. "Yeah, yeah. I guess that's *fine* too, but princes are so rich. If she married one, she'd never have to work again." She looked up at me with the intensity she reserved for her feelings about *work*. She knew the equation. I worked so we'd have the money we needed to not starve. To keep her in school. Even when it meant I didn't get to finish school myself. She didn't think that was fair. She thought Pa should be the one working. She thought the long hours I worked should bring in enough to do more than scrape by while holed up in a squatters' nest.

I couldn't fault any of that. But I didn't have any other options.

I could only do what was best for Nia. Maybe then she'd at least have a normal, comfortable life, even if we never got a fairy tale one.

I wiped the prickly heat off the back of my neck and let my hair out of its bun to redo it tighter again. The thick, ropey locks were straighter than Nia's, but otherwise she could have been a younger version of me, from the deep umber eyes to the tawny brown of our skin, sheened in sweat. Home was just down the alleyway up ahead, but getting inside wouldn't bring much relief from this heat. We certainly didn't have any air conditioning. I poked my finger through the hole in my T-shirt. It was about the closest to air conditioning I was going to get any time soon.

A siren wailed in the distance and the low hum of traffic and conversation filled the muggy air. The cauliflowers stacked in crates out the front of the local general store were wilted and smelly, but I still wished I could afford one. Or that I had a place to cook it. Or that Mom had taught me her recipe for zaatar roasted cauliflower before she'd left us.

A swarm of people bustled out of a subway exit, bumping around us. Nia's hand slipped out of mine, able in her small size to maneuver between bodies better than I could. I pushed through, grunting at the suited businessmen plowing between my sister and me, oblivious to anything around them.

A shoulder collided with my own hard enough to swing me and the charging body around toward each other, face to face. My eyes popped wide open.

"Rahanna?" A grin spread spontaneously at the sight of her, then faded as I took in what I saw.

Her eyes were wide too, in pure terror. A ghastly purple and red mark had spread across one swollen eye, vivid on her brown skin. She shook her head as though denying her own name. She cowered, pulled the hood she wore lower over her face and backed away from me into the crowd.

I stood motionless. *What on earth?*

"Zari? You coming?" Nia called out. She leaned against

the corner of our alleyway, waiting for me. "Hey, what's up?"

"I just … Go home. I'll catch up with you."

Nia didn't budge.

I pointed commandingly. "Go. Get started on your homework. I'll be back soon."

Nia groaned and turned around, shuffling off. I hesitated to let her walk the rest of the way alone, but it wasn't far. Then I ran after Rahanna. Had it really been her? With the split-second view I got of her and the black eye distorting her face, I wasn't entirely sure. But she'd seemed to recognize me.

The crowd cleared and up ahead, I spotted the young woman again. Her navy-blue clothing was scuffed and dirty, but still elegant and business-like, despite the oddness of the attached hood. She disappeared around a corner into a litter-strewn alleyway—a shortcut to Rahanna's family's apartment. I broke into a sprint.

The stench of old food abandoned in the trash burned my nose as I ran past overflowing dumpsters. My feet slid on something slimy. I steadied myself enough not to fall, and instead slammed into the back of the woman, grabbing onto her to avoid tumbling over entirely.

She shrieked, ducking away from me. Cowering against the wall, she covered her head with her hands.

Rahanna's doll-like eyes and pouty mouth were lost under injury and fear, but it was her.

A CAGE OF GOLD AND LIES

I spoke gently. "Rahanna? Hey, it's me, Zari. It's okay."

Her gaze snapped up. Her cheeks were gaunt, and her once beautiful coiled brown hair was matted and tangled. She cringed as an old newspaper blew past us, rustling. Everything about how she looked told me things were not okay.

She lowered her arms, staring at me for a long moment. "You didn't see me. Don't let anyone know."

"What? Why?"

Rahanna wrung her hands. "Can't let them find me. Can't let them find you. Can't let them …"

I grabbed her shoulder, trying to calm and comfort her. She twitched away and dropped to her knees, prostrating herself on the filthy ground. "I'll do it! Whatever you want. Please don't hurt my family!"

"What? No, I wouldn't!" I shot a worried glance at the people passing the end of the alley, but no one paid any attention to her outburst. *What is she talking about?* A shudder rattled her body and she turned to face me again, cheeks wet. My gut twisted at the mad horror in her eyes. Squatting next to her, I kept my voice soft. "I won't hurt you. You're safe now. Can you tell me what happened?"

"Can't ever be safe. No spellborn can ever be safe." Rahanna hugged herself as her shoulders trembled from chest-heaving sobs, then she blinked and shook her head firmly. She lunged, gripping my T-shirt in bony fists. "Did

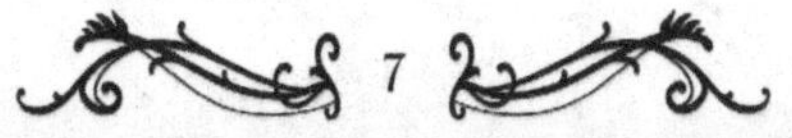

you tell anyone? What I can do? ANYONE?"

I gasped, but there was no threat in her action, only desperation. "Tell anyone what?"

Her voice cracked. "Magic. *Magic.*"

"No," I answered honestly. I didn't want people thinking I was a liar, or crazy, because what else would people think if I started saying magic was real? I hadn't even told Nia the connection between the magic and Rahanna's new job. She just thought Rahanna had gotten lucky.

"Good. Don't. You don't know. Can't know. Don't let anyone know you know," she rambled, her voice growing small. Her hands released and fell limply. She whimpered. "I can't be out here like this. They'll find me."

She crawled back to her feet and took off in the direction of her old home.

"Who?" I called, but she didn't respond, moving too fast. I chased after her. If she was in trouble, I wanted to help.

My mind raced, trying to understand what was happening. Rahanna was meant to be living the high life in her cushy job at the billionaire's estate, with balls, princes, fairy tale endings. She was meant to be the lucky one, but what had really been going on? What could make her this distraught?

I headed around the block, back the way Nia and I had just been. Rahanna tore ahead of me, barreling past other pedestrians. The apartment block came into view and she disappeared through a door covered in torn gig posters. I followed her inside, calling after her the whole way, but she wouldn't slow down. She took the steps three at a time. I caught up to her as she slammed into her family's door, knocking with her whole body as though trying to barge it down.

On the third bash, the door opened, and Rahanna's father stood there. A mix of emotions was still shifting across his face as Rahanna pushed through into the single-bedroom unit. He glanced at me, as though looking for answers. I could only shrug as I followed Rahanna inside.

"We have to go. Now. Now!" Rahanna stopped in the living area and doubled over, breathing hard. Moving boxes filled the space, some taped closed, others still open, bubble wrap and crumpled newspaper a nest for the belongings within.

"Hanna, dear?" Her mother put a dish back into the sink and stepped away from the kitchenette. She moved to hug her daughter, smiling under confused eyebrows.

Rahanna pushed her away. "No, now! Don't you understand? We have to go. We don't have any time."

"What's going on?" Sammy, Rahanna's brother, stepped out of the bedroom carrying a filled box. It dwarfed his wiry, tween-age body.

Rahanna let out a frustrated groan, as though we should all understand the situation. She turned to me, pleadingly, as

though I could help explain but I was as confused as ever.

I shrugged and told her parents, "I just found her on the street like this and followed her here. Something seems really wrong."

"I told you." Her mother's eyes grew fiery. "I said it was too good. It didn't seem right."

Rahanna let out a sob in reply. Her dad gave his wife a concerned look, then with a nod, grabbed a duffle bag from the corner and started shoving things into it.

Rahanna looked horrified. "No! No time to pack. Come on!" She pulled on her mom's sleeve, dragging her toward the door

A strange green light wavered in the air.

Rahanna rushed at me, pushing me toward her brother so that the two of us fell behind a stack of moving boxes. "Hide!" she yowled, looking pointedly between me and Sammy.

Scuttling into a sitting position, I pulled Sammy close and hushed him as his mouth opened. I didn't know what we were hiding from or why, but I knew I had to protect him, for Rahanna.

The light grew so bright it hurt my eyes. I squinted and noticed a crack between the boxes. I bent closer to peer through.

By the time my eyes adjusted, the green haze had mostly faded away. In its place stood three strangers in the middle of the small room. They wore matching suit-like uniforms, similar to what Rahanna had on.

All three of the men would have been huge and threatening even if they didn't just appear from out of swirling magic light. They had the air of Secret Service men crossed with grizzled Marines. One of them grabbed Rahanna and muttered something lyrical. Ropes appeared from nowhere, coiling around her like snakes. Magic. *More* magic. *Rahanna isn't the only one.*

She cried and pulled at her bonds. "Please, don't hurt them. Just let us go, and I won't tell anyone."

The closest man, scalp shaved like a neo-Nazi, held the magical ropes and shook his head.

Rahanna frantically thrashed, trying to free herself. "I'll do anything, give you anything. Just don't hurt them."

The neo-Nazi restraining her responded with a sick kind of pleasure in his voice. "You shouldn't have tried to escape. Everything that happens now is your fault."

"Let go of her!" Rahanna's dad shouted. He marched toward them, threateningly, bringing a solid arm up to swing.

The neo-Nazi spoke more rhythmic words I couldn't make out. Before Rahanna's dad could land his blow, a bolt of red light shot into him. He froze on the spot. His fist unclenched and he grabbed at his chest, choking, then collapsed to the floor.

My throat constricted. *What did they do to him?* I plastered

my hand over Sammy's whimpering mouth.

Rahanna screamed loud enough to cover the sound anyway.

Her mother fell to her knees, crawling toward her husband. She placed her hand on his neck, then chest, then face, trying to rouse him. "Why? Why? What's happening?" she wailed.

One of the other men stared down his nose at her. "All you need to know is that your daughter was disobedient, and this was the price. Nothing you've seen here is to be spoken of or you will pay a price again."

Rahanna crumpled, held up only by the ropes and the man beside her. "I'm sorry. I'm sorry." She repeated it over and over, her voice broken by sobs.

Sammy thrashed against me, and it took every ounce of my strength to hold him back. I bit down on my lip, suppressing the cry that threatened to reveal our hiding spot. A few seconds later, there was another bright light, and Rahanna's pleas ended.

The men were gone, Rahanna with them.

I let Sammy go. He rushed to his father, crying and trying to wake him up. Minutes ticked by as I watched, frozen in horror, as the man's skin grew pale. Rahanna's mom scooped Sammy away from the body, rocking him in her arms.

Nausea washed through me. Those men—they hadn't even blinked at killing someone. A father, right in front of his family.

A CAGE OF GOLD AND LIES

I wasn't supposed to be there. I wasn't supposed to know any of this. What would they do to me if they found out I knew about Rahanna, and magic? What if they found out I had witnessed the terrible crime that happened here, or that I knew Rahanna had been trying to run from something possibly more awful?

Rahanna's mom and Sammy were bundled together, lost in grief. The sorrow I felt must be a drop in an ocean compared to theirs. More than sadness, I felt fear.

I bolted. I didn't stop to say anything to Rahanna's family, nothing I could say was worth intruding on their anguish. I sprinted out of the building. I didn't slow down as I made the turn toward home. I had to find Nia and reassure myself she was okay. After what I'd seen, the whole world felt changed, dangerous. More than ever.

We'd assumed Rahanna was happy where she went. We'd never considered it could be worse than the life she'd left behind.

Magic might be real, but there was no such thing as a fairy tale ending.

ONE

THE ALARM WOKE me from a restless sleep. I reached over and picked up the phone I'd gotten from a charity, tapping at the cracked screen until the beeping stopped. Wiping my eyes, I confirmed the four AM start to the day. *I hate early shifts.*

Nudging Nia, I made sure she was awake before I crawled off the tattered mattress we shared. The nest of old blankets where my father normally slept was empty. He hadn't returned home last night, which meant he must be passed out on a street somewhere, sleeping off his drunkenness.

Sometimes, when I was in a dark mood, I wished Sergio would never come home. That it was just Nia and me. Times like last night, when he didn't come back, meant we managed a decent sleep without being woken by his night terrors, which only got worse when he drank. And this place was small even for two people. Still, I counted us lucky to have it—a fortunate find that had served us well for years. It was a blocked off room in a condemned building, where they had neglected to disconnect the water. Although the shower was broken, we had one sink and a working toilet in a small bathroom. The single, secure bedroom was only accessible by fire escape.

I headed into the bathroom, stripped out of my pajamas and changed quickly into my day clothes. Long, jagged cracks ran through the broken tiled walls, leaving bits of gray dust coating the floor and Pa's stinking floor-drobe. I kept my and Nia's clothes as clean as I could when using a tiny sink to wash them, and neatly folded in cardboard boxes by our mattress. I wrinkled my nose at Pa's mess but refused to touch it. I did enough work around here already.

My body ached from the poor sleep and I closed my eyes for a moment, trying to visualize myself into being motivated. Someday, I would live in a proper house with a real bathroom and washing machine. There would be a table where I could eat breakfast, a fridge, where I could keep fresh milk. It would have bedrooms for everyone so no one had to share.

As I headed back to the other room, Nia mumbled something and buried her head under the covers.

I tugged the blanket away, revealing her pouting face.

A CAGE OF GOLD AND LIES

"I know it's early. But you've got to wake up and get ready."

"Wanna sleep in. I can get ready and go to school on my own later."

I hesitated. She was twelve now, and she wasn't unfamiliar with being alone and independent when it was required. But if I left and took our alarm clock with me, it would be all too easy for her to sleep in and miss the breakfast Mrs. Hakim put on for kids of the community who didn't have it at home. And then she'd be going to school on an empty stomach, and Nia could be a super hangry kid. "Come on. I want you up now so I can drop you off at before-school care."

I tossed her clothes at her, then stuffed a package of expired instant noodles in my back pocket for my lunch break. Finger combing my hair, I pulled it back into a tight bun.

I slid the window open. From my perch, I peered out over the rundown slums of the industrial district to the towers of the CBD and then far beyond, where a beautiful estate with shining crystal spires crowned the mountain that loomed over the city.

Everyone knew about the Kings, the billionaire family who lived inside the famed Crystal Estate. They unofficially owned the city of Oramont. All the manufacturing and processing plants here in the warehouse district and half the high-rises in the rich areas were theirs. It was also rumored they controlled the government, police, and everything that

happened in this region. Most people thought it was the money that gave them power, but I knew it was the magic. Magic that silenced entire families, retrieved the escaped, and killed the unruly. Thinking about my childhood friend and the ugly way she'd lost her dad made a pain spike in my chest. How could anyone fight against power like that?

It had been three years since Rahanna's tragic escape attempt, but I still felt the fear as though it were yesterday. If anyone learned that I knew the truth, I didn't know what would happen, but I didn't want to find out. I'd seen enough of their power already.

I hadn't heard anything from Rahanna since that day. The spires of the Crystal Estate sparkled in the distance. *Is Rahanna still there? Is she still alive?*

Nia crawled through the window first then skipped down the clanging steps. I followed her outside and slid the newspaper-plastered glass into place.

Racing down the fire escape, I caught up with Nia. We walked together in the early hours of the morning, hearing the city waking up for the day. Moisture steamed off the pavement as the sun warmed the world. The general store owner's son was loading a delivery in and gave me a flirty smile as we went by. I pretended not to notice. He was nice-looking, with a tangle of curly dark hair and long-lashed eyes, but dating was something I didn't have the time or energy for, no matter how much part of me craved that sort of company.

Nia yawned loudly. It was too early for her to be up. She needed her sleep as much as she needed a good breakfast. Maybe I should have let her stay home until it was time to go to school. I felt like I didn't know what I was doing half the time, trying to raise her right, to keep her safe. I second guessed all my decisions. I hated when I had to work and couldn't be there with her. Nia thought I was overprotective, but she didn't know what I did about the world, let alone that magic was real and the consequences of it.

I only had a few memories of immigrating to this country. Even though I'd been ten at the time, I could only access fragments and flashes … running for our lives through dusty, broken streets, trying to escape the bombs and destruction and war-mad fanatics that wanted to kill us just for existing. Nia had been a newborn when we'd fled, spared even the vague, trauma-clouded memories. The one recollection that remained clearest was my mother handing Nia to me. She was just a tiny, almost weightless swaddle of blankets. Ma looked me in the eye and told me it was my responsibility to carry Nia, to keep her safe.

Sometimes I wondered if Ma was preparing me then for when she abandoned us, whether she'd planned it all along. She'd been gone six years now, and Pa had become just as absent in every way that mattered. He was either drunk or lost to a depression I had no resources to help him with.

I was all Nia had.

We reached the old hotel that had been converted into a community center.

"Do you think Mrs. Hakim has made manakish today?" I mumbled nostalgically, remembering the hot meals I'd eaten there myself before leaving school. A sharp pang of hunger tormented me.

"I hope so." Nia's eyes brightened. "Maybe you can come in and have some too?"

"You know I'm too old now." Wrapping my arms around Nia, I pulled her into a quick hug. She was well into her rebellious age and any kind of affection was a struggle, so I relished when she lingered in my arms for a few seconds. "Behave for Mrs. Hakim. If you don't, she might make you eat jigar again."

Nia cringed. "Eww, don't even mention it." She looked around, then dropped her voice. "You might put the idea in her head."

"Be safe. Love you!"

"You too!" She waved and raced into the converted hotel.

With a sigh, I turned and walked to my job at the cotton-processing factory. Since our immigration was less than fully documented, it was hard to find a decent-paying job. They knew I could only take cash, so they could pay me whatever pittance they wanted and I'd have to deal with it or miss out.

At least the public schools had to let any kids attend, regardless of citizenship status. It meant that Nia could complete high school. Then she'd hit eighteen and be in the same boat as I was in. But I have been saving up, so hopefully it would be different for her.

The walk to the factory was long but it saved money on public transport. I got there with just enough time to pull on the blue hair cap and white overalls required for the plant floor before my shift started.

The job was intense. Although the massive industrial machines did most of the work, human hands were required to do a lot of the actions the machines couldn't. Loading and unloading, hands and fingers moving fast between the metal wheels and arms, repeating the production line process over and over. I sometimes felt like a cog in the machine as well. Threading three rows of plying machines, I turned them on and watched the thicker cotton fly off the cardstock as it stretched out into a smaller thread before coiling onto drum-sized spools. The *whir-click-click, whir-click-click* of the machines always calmed my mind. I loved rhythms and had a knack for memorizing them. I hummed along to the beat of the machinery, keeping in the zone. Focusing on the sounds, I could hear there was a problem before the automated warning would go off. I could even fix it before it got too far out of sync with the others.

The machines had finished filling a few drums of thread, so it was time to roll them along to the next stage in production. Each barrel was taller and thicker than me, and although they were on coasters I had to put my shoulder into it to move the heavy cotton along the factory floor. The women in the next section gossiped as they locked off the last round of now-empty barrels.

"Did you see the photos of him on his boat? I don't think I've ever seen something so gorgeous."

The older woman scoffed. "Darian or the yacht?"

"Mr. King, of course!" The younger woman with badly bleached hair squealed softly. "I heard he owns this place. Do you think he'll ever do an inspection here?"

"Like he'd lower himself to our level." The older woman rolled her eyes at me as I pushed the barrel into position, as though we might share opinions about the Kings.

The blonde pouted. "But he is super pretty. I don't know about the other brother. I mean, he seemed sweet when he was younger, but there haven't been any photos of him for years. I've heard he's ..." I didn't need to see the politically incorrect hand gesture the woman made to know what she meant. People loved to gossip about how the older brother had become sick and disabled as much as they gossiped about Darian's good looks.

"Who cares what the Kings look like? I'd care more if they started paying us better and let us take proper breaks," the older woman continued. "Things were bad enough when Ronald King was still around, but since Darian's taken over he's stripped back all our workers' rights."

My face soured. The Kings were like royalty in our city and the news was always filled with their exploits. I didn't want to know. I avoided everything about them, as though distancing myself could make what happened with Rahanna no longer real. I left the area, but when I returned with the next barrel the women were still at it, becoming even more heated. "All your beloved playboy cares about is throwing his extravagant parties. He's making tons of money at our expense."

"Hey," the blonde grabbed me by my overall sleeve. "What do you think? The Kings are all right, aren't they?"

My lip twitched. What could I tell her? That I suspected the Kings were behind my best friend's kidnapping and her father's murder? I scowled. "There's no such thing as a good billionaire."

The older woman gave me an approving nod as the blonde let me go with a grunt of disgust.

"Stop talking and get back to work!" the foreman shouted. "If you don't, there are plenty of others who would be happy to take your spot."

I shrank away and scurried back to my machines, trying to stay out of the foreman's sight. I needed the paltry earnings too much to risk losing this job. Nia counted on me.

Several hours later, I prepped my section for the next shift. I gave a brief update to the woman who took over my station. She smiled as she read the displays. I headed to the office, had my inspection sheet signed off and collected my pay for the day. Before heading home, I detoured to the bathroom.

The moment I stepped through the door, an acrid smell burned my nose and someone let out a series of coughs then gagged. I recognized the scent immediately. The poor woman inside the stall vomited again as I grabbed a paper towel and wet it. After living in such a compact space with a drunk father, the sounds and smells of puke didn't bother me anymore.

The stall opened and Vera stepped out. I handed her the wet towel and she took it gratefully, wiping her mouth. She walked over to the sink next to mine and washed her mouth. "Zari, I feel awful."

"I'm sorry." I didn't know what else to say to the woman I'd never spoken to before. I only knew her name because we'd started working here on the same day. I generally avoided making friends, since most people didn't stick around here very long.

"I've been throwing up all night. There's nothing left,

but I can't seem to stop." Vera leaned over and rested her head against the white porcelain sink. "If I can't finish my shift, I'll lose my job. That's what happened to Karima last week." Vera turned on the faucet again and splashed water on her forehead. She looked pale and had a yellow-green tinge around her eyes.

I searched for the right words to say, but she spoke again before I could.

"Can you take my shift for me? I'm on the machines that strip the raw cotton. There's barely any supervision. The only time I see the foreman is at the start and end of my shift." Vera gripped the sink, her knuckles pale. "Say yes, please?"

"I'm not trained to run that section." I crossed my arms as I stepped back.

Her face paled several shades as she choked back another cough. "I can't lose my job. My car just broke down and I'm behind on rent. My kids and I could end up on the street."

Like Nia and I already were, for all intents and purposes. I frowned.

"The machine is all set up. You're smart. You should be able to figure it out by the time you need to refill it again."

"Okay." The word came out against my better judgement. If I got caught working a section I wasn't trained for to cover for Vera, we could both lose our jobs. But I understood her desperation.

"Great. I'll come back at the end of the shift and we can swap places before the foreman does the inspection." Instead of leaving the bathroom, she ran back into the stall and heaved.

Taking a deep breath, I reassured myself that I could do this, then headed out for Vera's baling machines. This shift wouldn't end until after school hours, and cell phones weren't allowed on the factory floor. I wouldn't get a break to call the school so Nia knew she'd have to walk herself home today. It wasn't unusual for me to run late when I had errands after work, but I always tried to let Nia know first so she wouldn't wait for me. I worried I'd made the wrong choice, already imagining a million bad outcomes for Nia between the end of school and when I would be with her again. But I had to trust Nia would be okay, now I'd committed to this.

Pressing the start button, I watched the giant mechanical beast jerk into motion. Metal combs flew so fast, I almost couldn't see them anymore. I watched and hummed along to the beat of the machinery, absorbing the patterns, learning the cues that meant I needed to assist the process. Five minutes later, I had the rhythm down. Time passed in a blink and soon Vera waved me down.

"Leave quickly! The foreman is almost here for the last inspection." Her color had returned, and she looked steadier on her feet. She took her spot at the machine, and I headed outside to wait for her while she shut her section down for the day. I sat on a broken concrete bench just down the sidewalk a moment before she appeared through the door.

Joining me on the bench, she smiled. "Thank you so much for that; you were amazing. No one suspected it was you instead of me."

In our matching caps and overalls we did all look alike out on the floor. Even the foreman mostly referred to us as 'hey, you.' People in power never seemed to care about telling their expendable laborers apart. I shrugged. "That section was easy enough to run."

"It took me a week of training to get up to speed there. You're too clever to be working in a place like this." Vera's eyes wrinkled as she looked at me with what seemed to be pity. She patted my leg. "I have to get going. Got to get dinner on for the kids. Thanks again."

"Wait a minute."

Vera paused, leaving her in an awkward half standing position.

"I'm glad I could help, but I don't work for free. No one does. I took your shift; I deserve the pay."

Her mouth opened as she looked down at me, a wrinkle appearing between her eyebrows. I was sure she was thinking about her budget, her busted car, her rent, her kids, that all relied on what she earned every shift. But I took a big risk to help her, and every bit of extra cash I could get meant my sister was closer to escaping the prison of poverty we were in.

I cut off any objection. "You got to keep your job like you wanted, but I get today's pay."

Several seconds passed as we stared each other down, then she sighed. "Fine." She reached into her tote bag and pulled out her cash for the day.

I tucked it away with the rest of my pay. "Pleasure doing business with you." Before she had the chance to say anything else, I turned and headed for home.

The streets of Oramont were never empty of desperate people or danger. I was anxious all the way home as the sun set around me and streetlights replaced its warm glow with sickly yellow. I hoped I'd find Nia in our room, doing her homework as she should be. I ran through my back-up plans for what I'd do if she wasn't there. *Check the school. Check Mrs. Hakim's.*

I vaulted up the fire escape stairs on tired legs. Climbing through the window into our small home, I let out a breath of relief to see Nia there, playing with an old, ratty rag doll. It was the one toy that had come with me from our old home, then it had quickly become Nia's as she grew into dolls and I grew out of them. Being twelve now, I hadn't seen her play with it for ages. Not that she had much else to entertain her. Guilt threaded through me, and my hand patted the extra cash in my pocket. It was tempting to put it toward something like a laptop or phone for Nia, but I had to keep saving up.

"You're home!" Nia sang. "It's late. I was starting to get worried."

"Sorry. I got a second shift." That was enough of an explanation. I shifted the side of our mattress back and ran my fingers over the crack of loose concrete in the wall. Pulling out the chunk, I stacked the extra pay on the stash of cash I hid there.

Pa was always at me for my earnings so he could buy more booze. Sometimes I'd have to give in and hand some over, just to keep him quiet, or keep him from getting violent. The only way I could save was to hide it from him. And I was saving for something important. I hoped to get enough together to buy Nia a fake ID and paperwork by the time she hit adult age. Then, maybe she could get a real job, with real benefits. Or even go to college. If I could get that for her, she could have a real life. She could be free.

With the money safe, I dropped onto the mattress next to her, exhausted. "You had an exam today?"

"Algebra. Nailed it. My friend Claudia said her dad uses math like that in his movie effects job all the time."

I smiled sleepily at her. I loved that she could dream about a career like that. She was clever enough that she could make it too. "And you've finished your homework?"

"I need to use the computer in the library for my English assignment." Nia set the doll down and looked up at me.

"We can go after school tomorrow. I'm not working." I ruffled her hair.

She hissed and leaned out of my reach while she finger combed it back into place. "Or …" Nia approached her words softly. "I could just leave school and get a job too."

"You're not old enough to work." I wasn't in the mood for this argument, one we had way too often.

"I'm almost as tall as you. I could pass as a short woman. Not like you have any ID to prove your age either." Her sight dropped to the doll as she spoke, and she picked it back up into her lap. "Then you wouldn't have to work so much."

Her intentions warmed my heart. She was already so responsible, but I couldn't let her make the same sacrifice I had. Because I'd made that sacrifice so she could have her childhood, her education, and hopefully more. If she gave up now, what was the point?

"No, you're going to get your high school diploma. Then … then we'll see." I hadn't shared my plans for my savings yet. I didn't want to raise her hopes until I had her documents in my hands. But school was non-negotiable. Pa had already tried to get Nia working too, wanting two daughters bringing in his drinking money, but I wouldn't let him. That had been one of our worst fights since Ma left.

A CAGE OF GOLD AND LIES

The sting of tears spiked behind my eyes, unexpected at the thought of her. How she left us with nothing more than a note saying, 'This is for the best. I love you.'

If she loved us, she would have stayed.

I let my anger burn away any chance of tears falling. I loved my sister, but sometimes it made me angry that I had to be the responsible one in the family. If Ma had stayed, I could have finished school. If Ma had stayed, maybe Pa wouldn't drink so much.

"One of these days, I'm going to be a boss bi—"

"Language."

"— and I'll make enough money for both of us," Nia vowed.

I smiled and reached for her hair again, but she dodged away.

"Don't treat me like a baby. I can do things. Amazing things. I wanted to show you. Maybe I could earn money with this somehow." Nia's fingers twitched at the rag doll, and it wobbled to life—without her touching it.

I stared. A tremor shook down my spine.

The fabric toy jumped up onto its feet on the mattress. The locks of yarn hair spun around its head as the doll twisted about, dancing across the threadbare blanket.

"See? Isn't this awesome?" Nia looked up at me, her eyes full of hope.

No. No, it couldn't be.

My heart pounded. It was just like Rahanna, being able to make small things move by magic. If anyone saw her doing this …if anyone knew …

"Nia! Stop that." I smacked the doll off the bed and it fell limply. Nia was … *spellborn*. That's what Rahanna had called it—she'd said that no spellborn could ever be safe. *Would they come for Nia? Would they sense her magic somehow?* I grabbed her shoulders. "Don't ever do that again. *Ever.* Promise me right now that you'll never tell anyone about this."

My reaction to her trick had startled her. Tears spilled and her lips wobbled.

I pulled her into a tight hug. "I'm sorry. But please, it's important nobody knows and that you never do this again." If they took Nia away, I didn't know what I would do. I remained there, holding her tight while I tried to calm my racing heart. I hadn't meant to scare her, but maybe it would keep her from doing magic again.

Nia sobbed as she looked up at me. "I promise."

I could hear the sincerity in her voice. But for the next few weeks, I spent every waking moment scared.

What if someone came and took the one good thing in my life away from me?

TWO

I WILL MURDER him for this.

Glaring at how the mattress lay askew over the floor, I pulled the corner away from the wall to confirm what I already suspected. My useless gene donor had stolen my savings. The loose chunk of concrete usually hidden by the mattress was now lying several feet away, and the small hole in the wall was glaringly empty. All my hard work and dreams had gone down the drain. I raced out onto the street, fury burning through me.

Sergio was at the second bar I checked, an Irish pub only a few blocks away. I stepped inside the dimly lit, dingy establishment, and heard his deep, raucous laughter. The only time he smiled these days was when he was drunk.

I knew he had problems. He suffered from depression and the nightmares of the war he'd fled. But he was supposed to be the grown-up. He was supposed to look after us, and his lack of concern for his daughters erupted a deep resentment that had grown over the last few years. I rarely thought of him as *Pa* anymore.

He sat on a high stool at the middle of the bar with several men sitting around him, all enraptured in whatever story he spun them. I walked up to him and shoved his shoulder. "Where is it? Is there anything left?"

"It'sss is my baby girl!" he crowed, waving me toward his surrounding drinking buddies. A smattering of loose change on the counter and the drinks all around answered my question for me. He picked up the last full shot glass in a row of empties and downed the clear alcohol.

I grimaced. "You've been here long enough. It's time to leave."

"But we're having s'much fun." My dad turned to the guys, and they all raised their glasses and cheered. I wanted to slap him. He'd wasted all my hard-earned money to be the center of attention for a few hours.

"Hey," a red-bearded drinking buddy jeered at me. "Do me one of your magic tricks! I want to see some magic!"

Panic seized my chest, quickly replacing the anger smoldering through me. "Some *what?*"

A CAGE OF GOLD AND LIES

"Yeah, show us an illuuusion," another crooned.

Why would they think I could do magic? *Please let them be talking about some kind of card trick.*

"I'm not a performer," I said. Slipping my arm under Sergio's, I tugged at him, but he didn't budge. Instead, he dragged me closer until I lost my center of gravity and had to grab the counter to keep from falling.

"Come on, do the—" He made a *phwoosh, phwoosh* sound. "Just wave your hands like you did this … whenever and make thingsss float about!"

I glared at Sergio. What did he know about magic? And what had he been telling these men?

I had to get him to shut up. This time when I pulled at him, he stood and took a few steps, then stopped as his face squished in concentration.

"Oh wait, it's the other one," he mumbled under his stinking breath.

My eye twitched. *He knows. He knows about Nia.* I was furious that in his drunken state he couldn't even tell his daughters apart. But I was also angry at Nia. She had promised not to tell anyone, to never use magic again. I thought she'd kept her promise. It had been months since she'd shown me and I was just starting to feel relaxed again, to stop worrying someone would spirit her away in the night.

Sergio's drinking buddies cheered and pounded their

fists on the bar, rooting for more beer.

"I've been telling them how m-daughter can do"—*phwoosh, phwoosh* again—"magic, but ..."

"Yeah. Sure. We all believe magic is real, right," I spoke quickly over him, rolling my eyes sarcastically. A few of the men laughed.

Fisting my hand into the front of Sergio's shirt, I pulled him out of the bar. The stupid man didn't realize what was at risk or the danger he was putting Nia in, boasting his daughter could do magic. Just saying it out loud might be enough for the wrong ears to overhear.

He didn't put up much resistance until we got outside. "I don't wanna go home." His bottom lip jutted out like a petulant child.

"I can't believe you! No wonder Ma left us. She couldn't stand to be around a useless drunk!" I crossed my arms while I glared at him, hoping he felt shame. It never worked. The alcohol always dulled his reason and emotions.

"You don't know what you're walking about ... talking about." His filthy finger waggled in my face. "I only started drinking to deal with the ... raising the ... you two on my own."

I growled at him, feral. What he was doing didn't begin to fall into the realm of raising children. Grinding my teeth, I chose my words carefully. "You stole the money I worked for and wasted it on booze. Don't you feel any shame?"

He waved a hand, dismissing my outrage. "You're my daughter, so you have own … I own … what you have is mine. It's all for the good of the family."

"You're deranged! You stole from me."

He shrugged, a smug smile like a challenge over his bad teeth. "Can't give it back. You shoulda hiding place better."

"I should be able to trust you!" My voice cracked with emotion. Our argument was starting to attract attention out on the street and I wouldn't let myself cry. Tension built throughout my body. I couldn't deal with him right now. Spinning on my heel, I stomped home, ignoring his whining as he trailed behind me.

He was right. I should have known. You couldn't trust anyone.

Regardless of why Ma had left, only one of us was now responsible enough to raise Nia right, and it wasn't him. I'd already given up so much to protect her. For years, I'd worked one crappy job after another. It was the only way I could keep her fed, even if it meant I went to sleep with my stomach growling. Everything I lost, everything I gave up, everything I missed out on would have been worth it if I could get Nia her documents. And Sergio had blown it. Nia had blown it. I was starting from scratch.

The familiar abandoned building came into view, and I

looked around, making sure no one was watching as I ran up the fire escape and in through the window. Nia was there, just putting her schoolbag down. She'd had to walk home alone because I had been out trying to find Sergio. Anger and guilt and pain churned through me.

I ignored Sergio as he stumbled and fell several times trying to follow me up the stairs. I slammed the window shut behind me then turned on my sister.

"What did you do? You promised me you wouldn't tell anyone!"

She was a deer in the headlights before my rage.

"About the magic," I hissed.

"I didn't … only …"

"Only Pa? How could you? You promised not to tell ANYONE."

"He was sad; I just thought it would cheer him up. It's only Pa. I didn't think it would matter."

"He just blabbed to a bar full of strangers!" I paced the few steps between both walls of the tiny room, then spun and stomped to the other wall. "Why would you do that? When has Pa ever done anything for us? I do *everything* for you. I've sacrificed everything!"

"I'm sorry! I didn't know."

"You did know because I told you! I told you not to tell. I told you to never do it again. You don't understand how dangerous it is! This is what happened to Rahanna. They took her away because she had magic. They killed her father when she tried to escape!"

Nia opened her mouth as huge tears rolled down her cheeks but the sound of our father falling through the now open window interrupted her. He let out a string of curse words, but we both ignored him.

I groaned out a sigh and sat on the edge of the tattered mattress. Pressing my face into my hands, I rubbed it for several seconds then pushed my loose hair back. "I'm sorry I snapped at you. It's just … I've given up so many things for you to have as much of a normal childhood as I can manage. I just want you to be happy and safe." My hand reached out for her, and she took it. I pulled her in for a hug, and we embraced each other for a long time.

The sound of a throat being cleared broke up the moment with my sister. Thinking it was Sergio wanting attention —he was petty like that—I turned ready to berate him again, and sucked in a breath of air.

A beefy man with soldier-short gray hair stood in the middle of the room. He wore a crisp black suit and rectangular silver-rimmed glasses, making him appear like an army grunt playing Wall Street dress-ups. He forced a smile that was more of a sneer as he looked around the messy space.

Oh no.

"Sorry to intrude," he said, not sounding sorry in the slightest.

"Zari? Who's that?" Nia asked.

I moved in front of her, hiding her behind me. My heart rate increased. Who indeed? And why? And how? And please not for the reason I'm dreading. My father sat on the floor, leaning against the wall next to the window he'd left open. But I hadn't heard anyone come in—hadn't heard steps on the fire escape. *It's magic. He came in by magic.* I tried to calm my frightened thoughts. Maybe he was from child services, or immigration enforcement, or some mundane organization that could also tear our family apart. I could find no calm. "What are you doing here? How did you get in?"

"My name is Mr. Shaw. I'm here on the behalf of Mr. Darian King. He has an offer for the daughter of Sergio."

My worst fears crushed down onto me. *No, no, no.* Was that all it took? One loudmouth yelling about magic in a public space? They knew about Nia. They must have followed us home. They were going to take her.

Panic rolled around inside me as I stared, speechless.

"Word of her talents have reached Mr. King, and he'd like to hire her for a job. The compensation would be very generous," Mr. Shaw continued, as though we needed clarification. Of course, he had no way of knowing I had experience with this sort of job offer before. That *talents* was his subtle way of saying magic. This must have been what had happened with Rahanna. Had it been Mr. Shaw who'd made her an offer in the beginning? Who'd taken her away the first time, when she'd been so happy to go?

As though the sound of *ca-chings* had woken him from his slumber, Sergio propped himself upright, splaying his hands out on either side of him so he didn't fall over. "She'll take it!"

I stood with my arms crossed, trying to temper my voice. "No, thank you. We don't want or need the job."

Nothing he could offer would be enough for me to let Nia get involved. I just hoped that a polite refusal would be enough.

"She's not know what she's talking about. We could use that money. She takes the job," Sergio agreed again, words slurring as he drifted down to the ground, eyelids fluttering closed.

"You don't know what they're offering," I snarled at him through gritted teeth.

Mr. Shaw ignored me, addressing Sergio instead as though he had every say in our lives. "Wonderful. I have transportation ready to take her now."

Nia gasped behind me.

"That's not happening," I told Mr. Shaw. I wouldn't let him steal Nia away, no matter what. I spread my stance, clenching my fists. I'd had my share of fist fights. Maybe I could take on this man.

He glanced over at us, ignoring my physical threat. "Please

reveal which daughter it is with the … talents, and we'll be on our way."

My jaw fell slack. Mr. Shaw didn't know which one of us was spellborn. Had Sergio never been specific in his bragging? I shot a look at him, worried he'd reveal Nia, but I didn't have to worry as a deep snore ripped out of him. He'd succumbed again to a drunken slumber.

"It's me. I'll go." I kept my face emotionless.

"Zari, no!" Nia grabbed for me.

I willed her to keep her mouth shut, to not reveal my lie. "I'll be back soon, I'm sure. It's just a job meeting." I lied through my teeth. Her face seemed so young, trembling and red with unshed tears. I put my hand on her cheek, hoping it wouldn't be for the last time. "Be safe. I love you."

"Come with me, please." Mr. Shaw gestured to the window for me to leave first. He didn't even give us a few minutes to say proper goodbyes, as though he didn't know this would be the last time we saw each other. I wanted to punch the glasses off his face, but I had to keep up the ruse.

I stepped out the window onto the fire escape, refusing to risk giving up the misdirection by looking back at Nia. I couldn't live with myself if they took her. The image of a ragged and terrified Rahanna flashed through my mind, but this time with Nia's face on my best friend's body. I'd do anything I could to protect my innocent little sister.

A CAGE OF GOLD AND LIES

Mr. Shaw stepped out after me, somehow looking professional and smooth despite the awkward motion. He closed the window behind him, and my chest clenched as I imagined Nia left all on her own without me, with nothing but a sleeping drunk as family. I looked down to the street, expecting there to be a car waiting for us, but didn't see one. It might be around the corner. Maybe once I was on the pavement, I could make a run for it. But that didn't end well for Rahanna. I had to get out of this some other way.

I stepped onto the first stair but stopped when Mr. Shaw cleared his throat. The moment I turned around, he pressed two fingers against my forehead. His cool flesh sent an icy shiver through me. Before I could back away, he whispered a few words I couldn't make sense of.

Nausea smashed into me, threatening to make me sick until I forced my eyelids shut. My body weighed a thousand pounds and then was light as air. Ice washed over my skin, freezing me into a motionless form. When I was on the verge of passing out, it stopped.

Opening my eyes, I found I was somewhere else, somewhere I'd never seen before. I lay on a bed in a small, simple room, not much bigger than the room I called home, but with proper furniture and a complete bathroom visible through an open door to the side. No windows. How did I get here? I remembered standing on the fire escape with Mr. Shaw, and then nothing.

The man looked down at me with a bored expression. "You fainted on the drive here. You have the night to rest. Your meeting to determine your career path will be in the morning."

Fainted? Yeah, right. I wasn't the type to faint. I questioned how I really got there, but I could already guess the answer. Magic. What had he done to me?

He held my phone in his hands, the phone that had been in my back pocket. Had he searched me while I was out? Stolen my stuff? I sat up quickly and the world swayed around me.

"Hey, that's mine!" I reached to snatch it off him but my body wasn't co-operating.

"No personal digital devices are permitted in these premises. Corporate secrets, you understand."

"I don't understand!" I snapped. "Just let me go. I'm not going to do magic for you. I can't!"

"Yet you know about magic and that it is the talent we have sought you for?" One gray eyebrow raised sardonically.

Ugh, damn it. I said the wrong thing. "I meant ..."

He adjusted his glasses and gazed down at me. "Until tomorrow." He backed away, closing the door behind him, and another loud click followed.

He locked me in. A drum pounded in my chest. I had to get out. I had to get back home to Nia.

It was a struggle to get to my feet, my body still woozy

and numb. I stumbled to the door and twisted the knob, but it didn't budge. I pounded on the door until pain burned through my hand, but no one came.

I was trapped. A prisoner. Because they thought I could do something there was no chance of me being able to do.

Mr. Shaw had said that tomorrow they would determine my career path. What was that supposed to mean? And what were they going to do to me, and Nia, when they realized I couldn't do magic at all?

THREE

THE *CLICK* OF the door made my eyes snap open. A round, red-headed woman in a simple gray outfit walked into the room. She carried a covered metal tray, and another woman in a matching outfit followed with a stack of gray cloth. I sat up from where I lay on top of the covers of the bed and watched them carefully, waiting to see what they did. The first woman set the tray on a small table in the room's corner.

"Ma'am, here's your breakfast and a change of clothes for you." She gestured to the other woman who placed the fabric on the end of my bed.

"Where am I?"

The women didn't even acknowledge I'd spoken as they left the room.

I shouted after them, "I want to go home!"

They didn't pause as the door clicked closed. I swung my legs off the side of the bed, wiping my exhausted face with both hands. Last night, after trying everything I could to get out of the room, I'd laid down on the bed for long, sleepless hours. My mind turned repetitive circles, wondering how I should approach this situation. Rebel or comply. Fight or plead. Lies or truth. I didn't have enough information yet to know what to do. Maybe it wasn't going to be as bad as I'd thought. Maybe Rahanna's situation was an oddity. Maybe *she'd* done something wrong, something deserving of what happened. *No. I don't believe that.*

Otherwise, why bring me here like this? Take my phone? Lock me in?

The aroma steaming from the tray made my stomach growl. How long had passed since I'd eaten a proper hot meal? I couldn't remember. I glared at it, wanting to pick up the whole lot and dash it against the wall.

I couldn't display my outrage though. I remembered all too well how Rahanna had looked and acted during her escape. Drawing too much attention to myself wouldn't end well. I needed to survive this so I could find a way to escape quietly, get back to Nia, then leave Oramont before these people noticed. And to survive, I needed to eat.

I climbed off the bed and peered under the metal cover.

A CAGE OF GOLD AND LIES

The plate underneath contained a bread roll, a single strip of bacon, scrambled eggs, and baked beans. My mouth betrayed me by watering at the sight. I sat at the table and used the fork to scrape everything up onto the bread roll and scarfed it down. It tasted so good I wanted to cry, from the feel of a proper meal hitting my stomach, and from the guilt that I could even enjoy it in this situation. Was Nia eating? Was she getting ready for school now?

I waited several minutes before I stood up, just in case my stomach refused the feast it wasn't used to. After the food settled, I checked out the delivered clothes. They appeared to be the same uniform the women had worn.

I didn't know how long I had alone, but I took the opportunity to shower and wash my hair. I wound it up into a bun, still wet, and put on the gray uniform. The neatly ironed slacks were just a shade lighter than the high-collared top that reminded me of a chef's shirt. I scowled at the ensemble, every instinct wanting to rebel against the implicit orders delivered with those clothes—that I was a servant now.

Despite the ratty condition of them, I folded my own clothes carefully and set them on the chair.

There was a rap on the door and a moment later it opened, with no confirmation of welcome from me required. Mr. Shaw stood in the hallway. A young woman in a uniform matching mine stood behind him, her face twisted and bitter.

"Ready? Excellent. Follow me."

Before I could say anything, he marched down the hallway to the next door, knocking again. It was opened by the person inside, an eager young man, who replied with a bright, "Yes sir!" when Mr. Shaw spoke the same command to him as he had to me.

The three of us followed Mr. Shaw like little ducklings.

The young man slowed down to walk beside me. "How cool is this?"

I glanced at him from the corner of my eye. He had neatly cut light blond hair that combined with his vivid blue eyes and sculpted physique to give him a rich, college frat-boy vibe. His eyes darted to me, and I looked forward again. This situation was anything but cool. But I didn't know what I could say to whom yet, so I just shrugged.

He continued on, undeterred. "When did you get here?" His friendly smile threw me off-guard. People didn't just smile at strangers. It wasn't normal. Not where I came from anyway.

"Yesterday."

We grew silent as we walked through a large foyer area with a white leather loveseat and two matching sitting chairs on top of a plush, snowy rug. A polished dark wood coffee table with an intricate gold design sat in the middle. My words fled me as I took in the grand room. The walls had so much art on them it was overwhelming. I imagined every piece hung there was worth more than I'd earn in a lifetime. Above me, the ceiling was high enough to have had another floor. Overall, this space was large enough for a few families to live in. What purpose could a room like this serve besides flaunting a person's wealth? It was such a waste when people were living off scraps in condemned buildings.

A large staircase appeared in front of us as we came around a corner, sweeping grandly upwards. Once we reached the next floor, the blond guy spoke again. "I'm Cam." He held out his hand to shake, and I stared at it, unmoving, until he gave up, but his smile didn't falter. "I got here yesterday too. Are you excited to work for Mr. King?"

"Anyone in their right mind wouldn't want to be here." The other woman glowered back at us, then faced forward again. She looked younger than me, maybe not even eighteen yet. Dark mascara streaked her pale cheeks, and her pixie-cut black hair was tangled and spikey. I suspected Mr. Shaw had brought her against her will like he had me.

"That's Lainey. I overheard her shouting when she arrived yesterday," Cam offered. "Don't know what bug is up her butt, but she better not blow this opportunity for us."

I looked between Cam and Lainey. One was possibly more determined to hate this place than I was, and the other was willing and eager to be here. Did they know more than I did about what we were in for? Or did I know more than them?

We passed a dining room and Mr. Shaw stopped for a moment, as though giving us the opportunity to look inside. The table was the longest I'd ever seen, and I counted at least fifty chairs before being distracted by the sight of a duster flicking through the air on its own. Several cloths also polished the long table without a single person touching them. Candelabras floated a few feet over the table while they waited for their spot to be cleaned. That was when I noticed the two servant women who stood against one wall, foreheads furrowed, and waving their hands.

"Mr. King has a few rules here, but the most important one is, you're forbidden to use any form of magic without explicit instruction." Mr. Shaw made eye contact with each of us before continuing on his way. Cam nodded eagerly. I stopped walking when an unmanned broom cut us off. It swept furiously, pushing the invisible dust out of our way. The place already looked spotless, yet the cleaners worked on.

We followed Mr. Shaw into another long hallway. This one contained floor-to-ceiling windows with intricate geometric frames holding the glass in place. Outside, a few men stood holding their arms out while their lips moved. A bright blue light glowed from their hands, but I couldn't tell what they were doing with it or what they were saying.

"Those men are maintaining the magical protection barrier. It's important you know that it encloses the entire grounds of the Crystal Estate," Mr. Shaw said.

"Protection barrier?" I couldn't help but ask. While I'd known about magic and seen it used once or twice, it hadn't been anything like that.

"It's an impenetrable shield that prevents unwelcome travelers from passing through, protecting the estate and those within it. It requires routine reinforcement." He began walking again.

"What he meant to say is it's there to keep us in, not keep others out," Lainey spat.

Cam rolled his eyes and shook his head. "Don't be so dramatic. Darian King just values his privacy and expects certain things from his employees."

The corridor opened into a large atrium. Another grand staircase stood opposite huge double doors. Metal adornments covered them and reminded me of something I'd seen in picture books of castles back when I was at school.

A woman and man stood facing a large, empty wall. They wore navy-blue uniforms, like Rahanna had worn, with large hoods over their heads. Several spools of colored yarn sat on the floor next to the wall, including one that looked like spun gold. Mr. Shaw stopped to watch them work, and we joined him. The pair whispered in a rhythm together, too quietly to hear the words.

"Ritualists," Cam hissed, excitedly.

"Huh?" I turned for more explanation, but that was when the magic started. Thin yarn spun off the spools, intricately knitting itself together like it was in a loom, invisible in the air around the threads. Gold quickly filled the wall with highlights of color. Before our eyes, the image of the estate appeared on the lines of the tapestry while it wove itself. The yarn flew back and forth so fast, it almost made me dizzy.

Taking a moment to reorient myself, I noticed the spools just as full as they had been before the magic started. Even as the tapestry continued, with more lines added running from one wall to the other, I couldn't believe what I was seeing. Within minutes, it reached from the ceiling to the floor.

Then I noticed the figure. They'd woven an image of a handsome man standing before the enormous estate building, a proud, strong expression on his golden face.

It was disgustingly beautiful. I didn't want to know how much something like that would cost to make with magic, let alone without.

Nia had made her rag doll dance. Rahanna had impressed me when she'd made her school textbooks flip through pages on their own. Then she'd worked out enough control to make her own hair dance around, similarly to the yarn, creating an intricate hairstyle she'd never been able to do herself. But this, this magic I'd just experienced, was so much more.

I couldn't comprehend how anyone could go from making

a doll dance to making a wall-sized woven artwork so detailed, I could see where the man parted his hair.

A quick look at the other new arrivals showed conflicting emotions. Cam stood with his mouth hanging open and amazement in his eyes. Lainey clenched her teeth while sneaking glances at the exits and security cameras mounted around the ceiling. Her hands were curled into fists, her knuckles white.

"Come on, now; we wouldn't want to be late." Mr. Shaw ushered Cam, Lainey, and me out of the grand atrium. We reached an elevator gilded in gold and crystal and went up five floors.

The elevator opened into a small foyer, with only one large door which led into an elegant, modern space. It was massive. Black leather furniture contrasted with the smoke-gray floors, and cushions and accessories created highlights of blood red. Several seating areas were carefully laid out with enough room to drive a car around. I'd only seen places this fancy in discarded magazines.

In the center of the room a man sat behind an enormous red and black desk. He was stunningly handsome; a perfect match to the figure woven into the tapestry.

This must be Darian King.

FOUR

DARIAN KING WAS jaw-droppingly gorgeous.

I'd heard the rumors. I'd seen photos in discarded magazines. But I wasn't at all prepared for the real thing. His perfectly coiffed caramel hair highlighted a skin tone with such a flawless healthy tan that it seemed to glow. He was perfectly proportioned with wide shoulders and a narrow waist. I was sure he wasn't much older than me. He wore a fitted black suit over a light gray shirt. Running down his broad chest was a blood-red tie, giving the impression he'd dressed to match his office. Looking up from some papers on his desk, he flashed a smile.

Unable to pull my gaze away from his god-like visage, I watched his every move as he stood and buttoned his jacket.

I'd never seen anyone like him before. It should be illegal to be that attractive. It was almost unnatural.

Something caught my attention as Darian moved around his desk. Another man sat in a wheelchair off to the side, hunched forward and leaning over like he didn't have the strength to sit up straight. His face was twisted and wrinkled in a way that created large folds in his skin, so I couldn't really make sense of his features. Was this the older brother everyone talked about? He didn't react to anything around him, barely even raising his gaze.

Mr. Shaw moved to Darian's side and gave him a small nod.

Darian clapped his hands together. "Wonderful. I don't think we've ever had three new residents in one day!"

Residents? He said it like they hadn't locked me in my room last night. Did he even know? Or were his underlings acting without his approval? Maybe I could get somewhere by appealing to him directly.

Darian patted Mr. Shaw on the shoulder, then focused on us. "I guess you want to know about your new jobs." Before any of us could reply, he leaned against the edge of his desk and continued, "I've recruited all of you to work for me personally. It's a real honor." He flashed a benevolent grin. "But first, we have to test your capabilities."

"What kind of test?" The words slipped out before I could stop them.

A CAGE OF GOLD AND LIES

Darian's eyes flashed to me, a hint of irritation there before he grinned again. "You're all here because you've proven to be spellborn, but I need to know what kind of magical ability you have. It's just a simple test to see how powerful you are. Your role at the estate and compensation is based on the results. So do try your best. I'm particularly interested if any of you are ritualists."

Cam stood up even straighter, as though desperate to be picked for the team.

We all waited silently as Darian walked over to a small table in the corner with a silver tray holding a dozen crystal bottles. After picking up a decanter filled with a syrupy amber liquid, he poured a little of the drink into a glass. The wide window behind him showed a view that looked down on the entire city of Oramont.

Darian returned to leaning his hip against the desk and took a sip. "Of course, all your needs will be provided for here, so I'll send your wages directly to your families."

Despite his welcoming tone, his words brought a chill to my bones. My imagination filled in the blanks between what he said. Our needs would be provided for here because we were to be kept as slaves. Our wages would be sent to our loved ones because we wouldn't be able to take it to them ourselves. The compensation sounded like a bribe to keep families from asking too many questions. Combined with the magical force field, and Lainey's ominous words about keeping us in … this really was a prison.

I glanced at Cam and Lainey. The sickened look on Lainey's face matched the feeling in my gut. Cam grinned and nodded. I suspected he came here voluntarily, buying into everything he heard with no reason to suspect the benevolence of this billionaire. But I was sure now. Lainey was right. Rahanna was right.

Apprehension crawled up my spine. Even if this *career* was great, I was going to fail the tests. I didn't have a lick of magical ability. I couldn't hide it any longer. I had to try to appeal to Darian.

"Mr. King, I'm sorry for the interruption, but I don't have any magical ability." Everyone's gaze shot to me, sending a prickling discomfort over my skin as I forced myself to continue. "Like, none at all. My father is a drunk and a liar. He's constantly boasting about things when he's at the bar, just for attention. That night, when he bragged about me using magic, it was all a dumb story. I think I should probably just go home."

Darian's smile disappeared, replaced by flattened lips. Pushing his hip off the desk, he took a few steps toward us. The crystal glass met his lips as he swallowed the rest of the liquid.

"Zani, is it?"

A CAGE OF GOLD AND LIES

"Zari."

His free hand rubbed his perfectly shaved jaw, then his lips widened again into a smile. "You don't need to hide your talents here. We know all about spellborn. You've seen the magic of our estate on your tour. It's not a secret you have to keep anymore."

"Yes, but …"

"Don't you understand what you're being offered? This is going to be life-changing for you. I know where you come from. That rat nest you call home. It's pathetic. Living in that level of squalor, constantly hungry, never clean. Disgusting. Why would you refuse everything I'm offering you? Everything I'm offering *your family*."

Lainey barked a harsh laugh. "Don't act like you're doing something nice for us!"

Darian raised his hands as though confused. "You should be honored by my offer. You should be on your knees, begging me for this chance to make your life of some value. I'm the only reason Oramont is such a successful city. If it wasn't for me, my businesses, my riches, many more people would be suffering."

Lainey took a step toward him.

Mr. Shaw blocked her path.

She yelled, "This is a prison! Your grunts hunt down every spellborn you can find, stealing them away to keep as your private magical slaves. Don't pretend we'll ever see freedom again!"

Cold sweat beaded all over my body. Taking Darian's pause as a chance to speak up again, I got the words out before I lost the nerve. "I'm sorry for the misunderstanding. I really can't do magic. Nothing at all. I shouldn't be here, so you should let me leave before I waste your time."

Darian blinked slowly and turned from Lainey to me with a sympathetic smile. "Every successful person fights cruel rumors, trying to invalidate all they've worked for. Just another way to know you're winning. Don't buy into her lies. Don't let her scare you into hiding your talents. There's so much opportunity for you here." He came right up to me, his stunning eyes shimmering as they seemed to shift from green to blue to hazel to gray. His lush lips curled up on one side.

I wanted to believe him. I wanted to believe he was good, that everything was going to be okay. "Promise me you won't keep us as slaves?"

Darian's demeanor changed completely. His voice grew loud and distorted. "Promise you? You? Who are *you* to be making demands? I owe you nothing and I'm offering you everything."

Cam spoke up, calm apologies in his words. I denied my magic ability again. Lainey screamed cusses. Darian hurled his crystal glass at the floor, effectively shutting everyone up. "Know your place! Every spellborn belongs to me, all of them! I own everyone and everything in this city!"

His face was mere inches from mine, his hateful eyes glittering down at me. "You will take the test. And don't you dare hold back to try to get out of it. I own you, and I own your magic." All kindness had left his voice, which was now shrill like a spoiled child's. "You will make yourself valuable in my service or you and your family will suffer the consequences."

FIVE

AFTER DARIAN'S OUTBURST, I kept my mouth shut. Nothing I said would convince him to let me go home. I wasn't even sure he'd let me go home when I failed the tests, which was inevitable. He was convinced I was spellborn, and if I didn't do magic, he'd just think I was withholding it. I shuddered and wrapped my arms around my chest, remembering how Rahanna's father had fallen lifeless to the ground.

After Darian's tirade, he'd ordered us to follow Mr. Shaw so we could begin our tests. I didn't know what to expect.

It was a short trip, straight down the elevator to some kind of sub-basement. We were taken past a number of rooms that seemed to be simple storage areas before reaching a

huge, industrial-style chamber with bright white lighting. At the end was another vault-like door with high-tech security, but our destination was in the center of the space. Lainey, Cam and I were directed into individual transparent testing cubes. They felt like prison cells. Several security cameras were trained on each of us.

The doors were closed behind us and we were left there with only one instruction: perform magic to the best of our ability.

Inside the testing space was a single small table with a few sheets of printed paper, and some random objects like thread, a bottle of water, and a dirty frying pan.

Reading over the papers revealed a collection of what seemed like nursery rhymes. Simple, short poems, with odd titles like 'To create a garment from a single bobbin' and 'To clean with but a single drop.' I didn't understand a lot of the words. They seemed old, like something from Shakespeare. *Are these spells?* I glanced at Cam and Lainey. They had the exact same setup. Lainey stood glaring at the spread, her hands clenching and unclenching into fists.

Cam paced, ran his hands into his hair and let out an exaggerated sigh. "Oh man, I thought you guys were going to completely blow this for me!" His voice was slightly muffled by the thick glass between us.

I shook my head at him. "How can you still want this?

After that tantrum back there?"

"You mean your tantrum or Lainey's? I saw a whole lot of tantrums happening."

"I mean Darian King saying he *owned us.*"

Cam shrugged. "You were being completely rude and out of line. You just riled him up, is all, and he's the boss. If you were a cadet, you'd get a hell of a lot worse chewing out by your drill sergeant."

"You don't understand what's going on here." I didn't know whether I really did either, but Rahanna had run from something, and paid the price.

"I know plenty. My uncle is in security here. He loves it. Says it's way better than being a cop—no red tape holding him back from serving justice. He came with Mr. Shaw to offer the job to me, and we talked over the whole thing."

I shivered, thinking about the kind of men who'd 'served justice' to Rahanna's dad. I took an involuntary step away from Cam. Clearly, his experiences and mine were so vastly different there'd be no overlap of understanding.

Cam bounced on his toes as though preparing for a boxing match. "I'm so pumped to be here, actually at the Crystal Estate! This is a damn good job, and the only place we can really use our magic freely and learn to get better at it."

"But I can't—"

Cam spoke over me. "You say you can't do magic, but

you must have some kind of potential for them to recruit you. What type of spellborn are you?"

"There are types?" I was so in over my head.

"Yeah. Three categories. Conjurers are your most basic. It's the way magic first presents itself, like making small stuff move on its own or simple illusions. Pretty useless tricks, generally they're not good for anything more than parlor magic and basic housekeeping. That's it for many spellborn, stuck as conjurers because they just don't have the power to cast spells." He tapped his finger on the paper at his desk.

I thought about how Nia's magic had first presented, making her rag doll dance. So she was a conjurer at least. "What are the spells for then?"

"For the ritualists. Those are spellborn with strong enough magic to be able to channel it with the help of written spells. They can't create their own spells, but there are plenty of existing spells that are really advanced magic." Cam picked up one of the sheets of paper, looking at it in awe. "Lots of spellborn have the power to cast spells right away, but sometimes conjurers grow into that power much later."

So the stolen spellborn all throughout this estate were a mix of conjurers and ritualists, and maybe a third type? Thinking back, the servants in gray uniforms like ours, doing the simple cleaning jobs had to be conjurers. They weren't doing anything elaborate, weren't speaking spell words, and were only using magic to control objects that already existed. The ritualists must have been the last two groups we'd seen—the men outside who reinforced the barrier, and the pair who created the elaborate tapestry in the foyer without using up any of the yarn. They'd spoken words. Spell casting, no doubt. And they all wore the hooded navy-blue uniforms, like Rahanna had. Maybe that meant she was a ritualist too.

"You said there were three types. What's the third?" I asked, distracting Cam from his reading.

"Oh, those are thaumaturgists. They are, like, once-in-a-generation rare though." He poked the paper he was holding in the middle as though he'd spotted something exciting. "See? This is why this place is so cool. You'd never learn about this stuff out in the world. You'd remain ignorant, like you are now."

I bristled. But it also made me wonder about Nia. She'd displayed magic at a much younger age than Rahanna had. And Nia was certainly younger than the three of us here. Did that mean she'd be powerful? With the right teacher, she might end up even stronger, be able to do amazing things. Was there a school for spellborn children out there somewhere? Was there anything out there for spellborn other than this prison?

Cam looked at me with a grin and shook his body as though loosening up. "I'm pretty sure I'm a ritualist. I mean, I've never gotten my hands on a real spell before now, so I don't know, but I can just feel how powerful I am. That's what this test is about—why they've given us some spells to try. Either we cast them and are ritualists, or we just do some other little trick and we're conjurers. Moment of truth."

With a deep breath, Cam picked up the bobbin of thread and spoke the words of the spell written on the page. As the chant crept out of his mouth, the blue thread shot off the bobbin and spun in the air. It danced around, crisscrossing with itself until a form took shape. I looked back at the bobbin, but there was still more thread on it, as though it were never ending.

I'd glanced over that same spell, but hearing it spoken aloud, hearing the rhythm of the poem, stamped it indelibly into my mind.

"From clew to clout,

Appetency bethought.

Behold from aught,

A raiment wrought."

Within a few minutes, there was a striking blue suit jacket hovering in the air. Once the last stitch finished, the garment laid itself on the glass table.

"Yeah!" Cam punched the air. "Nailed it!" He waved at the security cameras, then did a little victory dance.

Two attendants in gray uniforms appeared from down the hall within seconds. *They must be watching our every move.*

A CAGE OF GOLD AND LIES

They unlocked Cam's cell and went in, quietly discussed his tasks, then nodded. They led Cam out and locked the room again. Cam grinned from ear to ear as he followed them away. Almost as an afterthought, he yelled back, "Good luck!" Then he disappeared around the corner.

Luck wasn't going to get me anywhere unless I could luckily get instant magical powers.

Maybe I could though. Maybe I already had magic and just didn't know it yet. I should at least try and cast a spell. Creating a garment from thin air seemed way too daunting, but making something clean might be easier. Refocusing on my sheet of instructions, I rehearsed the rhythm in my mind for a few minutes.

I'd only spoken the first two words aloud when Lainey snapped, "Thought you couldn't do magic."

I shot her a look and finished the spell words … and nothing happened.

Nothing.

Not even a twitch or spark.

I hid my disappointment under a snarl. "Well, obviously not. Guess I just thought it was worth a try." I had to. It might have been the only way to save my skin, to save Nia. *What do I do now?*

Lainey came right up to the edge of her cell, close enough that her breath steamed up the glass when she spoke. "It's

not worth a try. Don't buy into their game. This place will eat you alive."

"I know," I whimpered, panic taking over. I moved close to Lainey, and spoke softly, unsure whether we were being recorded as well as watched. "I had a friend, a few years back. They took her away, killed her father."

Lainey's panda eyes softened. "You really do know, then. Damn. Sucks to be us."

"Did you … who …?"

She hesitated for a long moment, chewing her lip. "My brother."

My belly clenched. I could hear the pain in her voice. "What happened?"

Lainey's mouth twisted wryly. "He came here, as full of stupid optimism as that blond chuckle-head, Cam. He really wanted to learn more, cast real spells, but he was only a conjurer. He kept collecting spells anyway, just in case. That's not allowed, by the way. Conjurers don't get access to spells. Even ritualists only get limited access, depending on their clearance."

The inevitable tragedy at the end of her tale felt like it was crawling its way up my spine with sharp talons. "Was he … punished?"

"Oh, there's still more. When Ethan, my brother, came here, we already knew I had magic too, but decided to keep it quiet because I was young, and it was only just developing. But Ethan thought it would help me to get learning early. He worked out a way to send the spells he collected to me in secret. That's even more not allowed. *Really* not allowed."

Lainey knew so much about how things worked here already, and that explained it. She'd been in communication with her brother the whole time. Forbidden communication.

"Then it was punishment time. Darian found out. He sent his thugs to use me and my parents as a lesson for Ethan. Mom and Dad … it all happened so quickly. And then I screwed everything up even worse." Tears rolled down her face as she spat out the words. "I used one of the spells Ethan had sent me to try and fight back. Then they knew I was a ritualist. Better than my basic brother. It wasn't worth keeping him—not after they got a hold of me. Ethan's only value then was being an example so I'd learn my place."

She didn't need to spell it out. I knew how they made examples. *She lost them all.* My nose stung as tears of sympathy pushed to the surface. "I'm so sorry."

Lainey swiped her eyes and shrugged. Her teeth bared, feral as she spoke. "Nothing matters anymore." She turned toward the cameras and made a rude gesture. "I'm going to get you back, you bastard! I'm going to twist your head off your body first chance I get!"

I tensed, but no one came running to punish her. Maybe

we weren't being listened to.

Lainey picked up the papers and ripped them into pieces, throwing them like confetti. Then she swiped her arm along the table, throwing everything off it onto the ground. With a final sigh, she laid on the floor, hugged her knees to her chest, and closed her eyes.

How was I going to survive this? If my life didn't have value to Darian, if I had no magic, if he thought I was lying, if I looked at him wrong, it could all be over. Once they got rid of me, it wouldn't be a stretch for them to work out it was Nia all along with the magic, and then it would be her, here, in this hellhole.

I have to keep trying. I have to be able to do something.

Besides, if my sister had magic, maybe I did too. Lainey and Ethan both had it. Maybe it ran in families.

Taking a deep breath, I returned my attention to the cleaning spell.

"Hie droplet,

Moil shall we taunt.

Thrice a scullion's hand ye be,

Orts and grime avaunt."

I read over the lyrical words and stared. Again, nothing happened.

I didn't need the paper anymore. I'd learned the spell easily after the first repetition.

I tried saying the words while holding the dirty pan. I tried saying the words as I poured a drop of water onto it. I concentrated my every thought onto the spell.

Nothing.

I gave the other spells a go, just in case.

Nothing.

On a growl, I hollered out the words, hoping I could infuse the spell with frustration to give it the push it needed. Anger, desperation, and weariness all washed through me as I tried again and again. The words of the spells etched into my mind and soul.

And still, nothing.

I couldn't give in. I recited the rhymes for what felt like hours. Lainey rolled over, snoring softly in the corner of her cell. I took a short break, trying to clear my head, bring back some focus, then started again. I tried to do simple magic like Nia, making something move on its own. Even a piece of paper. Even a mote of dust. They wouldn't co-operate. My stomach howled in hunger, telling me I'd missed more than one meal. My mouth was dry and I drank the water meant for the spell. I was sure the sun must have set by now, somewhere far above me. Thoughts of Nia coming home from school to be alone without me kept me going. I thought I would send myself mad with the repetition when a voice interrupted me.

"Why haven't you cast a spell yet?"

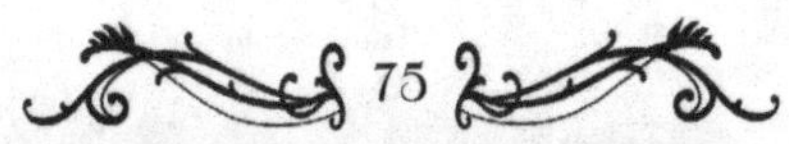

There was a man in the cell with me.

Except there wasn't. He was only partly there, ghostly and transparent. I stared at him blearily, my mind still repeating the spell words of its own accord, too absorbed in them to consider what was right in front of me. Was I seeing *a ghost?* I didn't even have it left in me to be startled, but I was lost for words.

"You've been at it all day. Either something should have happened already or you should have given up." His features were hard to make out, smoky and amorphous. He floated around me as though inspecting the table of props.

"I … I can't give up."

He turned to inspect me then. His face shifted and changed. Sometimes I could almost see his eyes narrowed on me; sometimes he was less than a puff of breath on cold air.

"Are you a ghost?"

There was a faint wisp of a shrug. "I think so. No one can hear or see me unless I want them to, which I don't often. It usually causes more problems than it's worth, what with all the screaming and fainting. You're taking it quite well."

Did he just smile? It was hard to see. If I was handling this well at all it was because I was too confused to be shocked, but the confusion was wearing off. On the verge of a hysterical laugh, the ugly kind that would make everyone question my sanity, I swallowed it back. If magic existed, then why couldn't ghosts? For all I knew, it was common. I looked up at the surveillance cameras trained on me, wondering if whoever monitored them was seeing what I was.

The ghost's eyes trailed after mine. "They can't see me on the video surveillance either. This is our little secret," he whispered.

A little of that hysterical laughter burbled out. I glanced over at Lainey, but she hadn't budged in hours. Just me and a ghost then. I could probably start screaming, wake up Lainey and get security to see what the fuss was about, but the ghost wasn't being threatening at all. Didn't mean I could trust him though.

"Who are you?" I asked.

A shimmering ripple rolled through the ghost's smoky figure. "You still haven't answered my question yet. Why are you trying to cast a spell you clearly can't? These are simple spells. Any ritualist should be able to do them. Just give up and do your conjurer trick and be done with it. Why keep trying to prove you're something you're not?"

Frustration got the better of me and I slammed my fist on the table, making the empty water bottle tip over. "I'm not trying to get a better job! I'm not even a conjurer. I'm not spellborn in any way. I have no magic!"

There was a long, floaty pause. "Then why are you here?"

He sounded honestly curious. I had no idea who he was,

but he'd said this was our secret, and I found myself spewing out the story that led to me being stuck in this glass cube. I recounted how my drunken father had told the entire bar his daughter could use magic, and how Mr. Shaw had appeared, demanding I go with him. I didn't mention Nia, but told the ghost about the threat Darian had made when I'd pleaded with him and explained that I couldn't cast spells.

"So I have to. I have to cast something, *anything*, or …"

"I can cast a spell for you."

His casual words shocked away the sob that had built in my throat. "What?"

"I'll cast something for you," he said again, softly. "It would be easy. Then they wouldn't hurt your family."

I shook my head, gaping at him. Was this a trick? Some part of the test? A trap laid by Darian to see if I was trying to cheat? "Why would you do that? You don't know me. Why do you care what happens to my family?"

He seemed taken aback. "Why *wouldn't* I?" His spirit hands raised like scales. "Cast a simple spell that costs me nothing, or don't and let someone be hurt? It's not a tricky dilemma."

The offer was too tempting, too worrying. "What would it cost me?"

"Cost you?"

"What would you want in return?"

The ghost cocked his head to one side. "I don't know

what kind of life you've lived, but you clearly have some trust issues. Sometimes people do good things just because it's the right thing to do."

"If that was true, I wouldn't be here right now." The retort flew out of my mouth. "People don't do things for others out of the kindness of their hearts."

Instead of the angry response I expected, the ghost shrugged. "I can't change that, but I can cast a spell for you. So, which one do you want?"

I thought about what he'd offered. Could this really work? Was this the miracle that was going to save me from failing this test? But then what? Looking over the tasks on the sheet, I wasn't sure I could ask for any of them. If the ghost cast a spell from there, it would appear to Darian that I had a full ritualist's ability. Then I'd be expected to be able to do it again.

I had to ask for something else. Something a conjurer might do. Something useless, like Cam had said. I had to prove I was truly, utterly useless, then maybe I would be let go. Or killed, like the useless conjurer Ethan. My lips twisted at the thought, but I pressed them firm. If that was the outcome, then so be it. Hopefully, my sacrifice would at least be enough that they wouldn't go looking for Nia.

I had to take a chance with the ghost. "It's a deal. But only if you tell me what you want in return, and you must want something. I don't believe this is just you being kind."

Ghost groaned dramatically. "Maybe what I want is not letting someone suffer when I can easily prevent it?"

I folded my arms across my chest and waited.

"Well, it should be easy but you really want to make things difficult, don't you? Fine. I don't know. How about I ask you a riddle? If you can answer it correctly, then I'll cast a spell. It'll be like you've earned it, instead of me doing you a favor."

My face scrunched in confusion. "A riddle?"

"Yep. Indulge me. I haven't talked to anyone for a long time. This will be fun."

A cold sweat beaded up the back of my neck. Was this some kind of ghost trick? What if I couldn't answer it and lost the deal? I didn't have any other option though. "Okay, let's do this."

Ghost almost seemed gleeful. "Yes! Right, so here it is. There were thirty wolves in a field, and twenty-eight sheep. How many didn't?"

I blinked. "Didn't … what?" Thirty wolves, twenty-eight sheep … I couldn't work out the equation or what he was asking. I couldn't even think where to start solving it.

Ghost's grin became clear. "Thirty wolves, and twenty"— He winked at me, pausing emphatically—"*ate* sheep. How many didn't?"

"You just told me the answer!" I snapped, confused and

somehow insulted. He didn't even give me a chance to work it out myself.

"Which is?"

"Ten didn't eat sheep! That's … that's dumb! That's not a riddle; that's like a dad joke." What was he playing at? He wasn't taking this seriously at all.

"Aw, come on. I thought it was a fun one."

Who was this guy? This was not a *fun* situation. This was life or death. But maybe, since he was already dead, he could only care so much.

"Whatever," I grunted. "I got it right. That was our deal for your payment, so now I want you to cast a spell exactly as I tell you to." I hoped he could do what I had in mind. I wasn't sure what magic he was capable of, or what magic in general was capable of, but I had a plan. Fingers crossed it would save my life, and Nia's too.

I just hoped I wasn't somehow indebted to this ghost for something more.

SIX

THE CREAK OF the glass cell door sliding open announced Darian's arrival.

His striking appearance sent shivers arcing through me. I hadn't expected him to come personally when I'd waved down the security cameras. I'd thought it would just be the same overseers who checked Cam's work.

"You've taken all day!" Darian stood outside my cell, arms crossed while he glared down at me through the open door. Mr. Shaw stood behind him, taking notes on a touchscreen device.

I gaped, still shocked at his presence.

He waved his hands, a *get on with it* gesture. "I hope you have something impressive to show me."

Darian's booming voice woke Lainey from her defiant slumber in the cell beside mine.

"I couldn't cast any of the spells." The words squeaked out of me.

Darian's face grew red and his gaze violent.

"But I did this!" Holding my hand out, I revealed the bobbin of thread that had been blue before, now a shimmering gold.

Darian's eyebrows shot up as he moved into my cell for a closer look.

I stammered out the words I'd rehearsed in my head. "This is it—this is the only magic I've ever had. I didn't want to admit it before because it's so useless, it's embarrassing."

"Useless—?" Darian reached out, and the second he touched the bobbin the thread returned to the previous sky-blue color it had been before the ghost worked his spell.

"That's why. I can only change small things, and the moment someone other than me touches them, they revert back. That's why I couldn't even use it to help my family be richer. It's completely useless." I chewed my lip, hoping he bought the story. If the magic was only temporary, barely more than an illusion, I hoped Darian wouldn't try and make me use it ever again. Lainey watched on as well as I explained my 'magic,' a small frown on her face.

Darian snorted a derisive laugh and tossed the bobbin of thread away casually. "You're right. That's probably the most useless magic I've ever witnessed. Even if it stayed gold, I'm a *billionaire*. You couldn't possibly fathom the extent of my riches. My watch is more valuable than your little trick." Darian flashed his wrist, admiring his shiny timepiece and clearly expecting me to do so as well. He tilted his head up so he could stare down his nose at me. "I thought you'd be more useful, considering who you are."

His words lingered in my mind. Because of who I was … what did he mean by that? I was a nobody, especially to someone like him. He left my cell and turned toward Lainey, looking her over resentfully as her door slid open.

I scrambled out more words before I lost the chance. "I can't even make things move about on their own. So, you see, there's really no point keeping me here. Can I leave now?"

He turned back to me, a glint in his eyes. "Can you leave?" Darian shook his head, then gave a mocking laugh. "What are you—dense? I told you already. I own *all* spellborn, whether they're useless or not. You never know how magic might develop, and even conjurers with the most pathetic powers have their place." He spat the word *conjurers* like it was filth on his tongue. "I'll just have to find a place for you equal to your worthlessness."

His words sent shame flooding over me, threatening to make me drown. I *was* worthless, but it wasn't my fault. At least I recognized that after years of self-hate. I was a victim of circumstance, born to a family who'd barely escaped a war-torn country. I scraped by every single day to make sure we survived another night. I refused to lay down and die no matter how hard poverty tried to crush us. I'd given everything for Nia, and without me, she'd be lost. I'd never stop fighting for her.

Desperation balled my hands into fists and fury tingled in my arms as I prepared to strike Darian. I would fight claw and tooth to get free of him.

But before I could, Lainey stepped out of her cell, shouting at the top of her lungs. "I was right. No matter what we do or don't do, you're keeping us as your slaves." The vein in her forehead bulged as her face reddened. Tears traced down the existing black lines on her cheeks.

I should have known too. No way would they tour us around this magical estate, let us see everything that happened here, and then let us go again. Mr. Shaw had been careful to hide any mention of magic on my first night, talking about talents and saying I'd fainted, up until the moment I let slip the M word myself. They wouldn't let these secrets get out. The moment I saw any of this I should have known I'd never be allowed to leave. *It was stupid of me to hope.*

Mr. Shaw moved in closer, but Darian didn't seem threatened at all as Lainey approached him. He eyed the trashed cell she'd left. "And you've clearly done nothing other than disrespect the space and equipment provided to you."

"*Respect?* You disgust me. I would claw my own eyes out before I respected you. But I'm going to claw yours out first." Lainey growled.

Darian lifted a hand. "Watch your tone. I should make it clear—resistance will be swiftly penalized. Defy me, and your family will suffer."

Her voice grew shrill and hysterical. "You don't even remember? Do you destroy so many families you can't keep track? You already slaughtered my parents and my brother. I have no one left in this world!" Her head hung down, and she swiped her face with her palms. When she spoke again, her tone was low and determined. "I have nothing left to lose."

The words burst out of her as she sprang forward. Her voice echoed through the room while she cast a spell, throwing her arm at Darian.

"Fane my flesh,

Brawn, this orison bestows,

Wrought stalwart mine heart,

And strengthen mine blows."

A swirl of golden light whipped around Lainey as she brought her glowing arm crashing down into Darian's chest.

He didn't even flinch. A disturbing, crunching sound came from the impact point as Lainey seemed to hit an invisible barrier surrounding Darian. Lainey cried out briefly as the air was visibly smashed from her lungs, her chest caving backwards. She was flung against the glass wall of the testing room, then slumped forward. She convulsed in obvious pain and dropped to her knees.

Darian smiled, unfazed and untouched by her attack.

I ran toward Lainey, my every instinct to go to her, help her, even fight with her. But Mr. Shaw blocked my way out of my cell. He wrapped a huge hand around my upper arm, holding me in place. I tugged fiercely, but couldn't break free. He gave his head a single shake of warning.

All I could do was watch as Lainey forced herself painfully to her feet again. Her lips were bloody.

Another spell danced from her mouth, the lyrical words burning into my brain as she worked her magic.

"Gyve of the turnkey,

Malison to the nithing.

Forfend escape,

Dight in seizing."

Ropes appeared from nowhere, encircling Darian, just like I'd seen happen to Rahanna. These had to be the spells Lainey had told me about, the ones her brother sent to her. Ones that ritualists under Darian's control used to capture and kill people.

The moment the ropes touched Darian, they vanished in a flash and re-appeared around Lainey, three times as thick, three times as many, constricting her three times as tight. Her skin grew blotchy and her eyes bulged.

"Give up already," Darian mocked. "You can't touch me."

Lainey writhed in her bindings, growling and grunting. "No! Never! I'll kill you!"

With a bloodcurdling cry of defiance, her body levitated off the ground. She glowed and energy crackled through the room, making my hair stand on end. She had so much power, I could feel it condensing the air. I prayed that she would win, but my heart only held fear.

From within her rope cage, Lainey howled her spell.

"Behoove mine heart,

A sanguinary desire,

Rend foe apart,

Till last breath suspire!"

The wrongness in the air slid across my skin as it sought its prey. A *crack* echoed through the room, and it was Lainey who screamed. Bloodcurdling.

I shut my eyes.

I didn't want to see it, didn't want to be here. I dropped to the ground and Mr. Shaw let me fall. I wrapped my arms around my knees, hugging them to my chest. This was all a terrible nightmare. I was still at home with Nia, on our ratty mattress in the condemned building we called home. We'd probably stayed up too late talking about Rahanna and fairy tales. If I dug my nails deep enough, the pain would wake me. Nia would be softly snoring next to me, just the two of us, safe, together.

Ear-piercing wails dragged me back to this awful reality—one where I couldn't grasp how everything that happened could be possible. Broken by the horrible sound, I opened my eyes and saw Lainey collapsed awkwardly on the ground, her body struck over and over as though by an invisible blade. Blood pooled and sprayed around her.

The screaming finally ended. Her skin grew abnormally pale, then her head rolled limply to one side. *Is she ... is she gone?*

I wanted to run to her, shake her, see her eyes open and find out she was still alive, but it was too late. Whatever magic she'd attacked Darian with had killed her instead. Her body lay in torn pieces, and her chest didn't move.

Behoove mine heart,

A sanguinary desire,

Rend foe apart,

Till last breath suspire.

Lainey's final words echoed through me like a haunted melody, words of a girl now dead. Words I wished I didn't remember but knew I'd never forget.

Darian sighed as he squatted next to Lainey's limp form. "Such a shame. I hate that it had to end this way." He dropped his head for a moment, like he was honoring her death with a moment of silence. The fakeness of the gesture wasn't lost on me. He always had to put on a good show, even if those watching didn't believe it. As though he believed his own lies enough for everyone. "I offered her my generosity. I did my best to show her the right way, but she was too stubborn to see it. So much natural talent and even more potential. I hate to see such a great resource go to waste. It's a pity."

He stood, taking a moment to give me a hard look. A silent warning of what might come.

"Deal with all of this," he instructed Mr. Shaw with a dismissive flick of his wrist, and he walked away. As though *all of this* was nothing.

Lainey wasn't a broken toy to clean up. She'd been a unique, valuable person. One I'd be sure to never forget. I'd honor her memory when I found a way to escape. I'd let her death give me strength when the moment came. If it ever did.

Through my grief, horror and tears, the world seemed barely a dream as Mr. Shaw dragged me to my feet. He yelled at someone to clean up the mess. He dragged me away from Lainey's broken body. From every part of her life Darian had cared so little about destroying.

I sank further into my despair. The fight between Lainey and Darian replayed through my mind. The bloody images of Lainey torn apart by her own magic were seared behind my eyes. It was as though every spell she'd cast at Darian had bounced back onto her.

How had he done that? Was there some kind of counter-spell? His mouth had never moved, so he hadn't cast anything. But he'd known he was safe; right from the beginning, he'd known how it would play out. His confident, mocking smile had never wavered. He must have some kind of magical protection, and it must be there all the time.

No one could use magic to hurt him. If that extended to physical attacks, no one could touch him at all. There'd be no fighting him. No stopping him. No getting away.

Darian really did own everything and everyone he wanted.

SEVEN

I DIDN'T ARGUE when Mr. Shaw told me to follow him. There was no point fighting. I wouldn't win. No one could against Darian King.

Mr. Shaw kept a steady pace before me. Still in shock about the death and horror I'd just witnessed, it took a while for me to take in my surroundings.

We'd left the main building and were walking along the edge of manicured gardens on a perfectly maintained stone path. Just like everything else here, even the grass didn't dare stray where it didn't belong. The pea gravel between the stepping-stones seemed individually polished.

Night had fallen while I'd spent so many futile hours trying to cast a spell. I wasn't sure what time it was, but garden lights sparkled around me, brightening our path under the starry sky.

The main building of the Crystal Estate was to my left. The glossy, crystalline walls, glowed in the night. The artistry of them was incredible. Hands and technology alone couldn't have crafted anything like it. Magic was used for this architectural wonder. The walls loomed over me, oppressive.

The ritualists I'd seen earlier strengthening the barrier to the outside world weren't there today. I guessed it was something they did routinely, rather than all day, every day. I followed Darian's lap dog and tried to push the pain from Lainey's death far away.

Someone scurried past nearby on another path. A woman in navy blue with coiled dark hair puffing out from the hood over her head. Her brown eyes darted to me, and she slammed to a halt for a moment, terror on her doll-like face as she took in my appearance.

Rahanna. My heart cried out to her. But I was smart enough to stay quiet.

She turned away abruptly and sped off, disappearing through a door with the briefest of second glances back to me. Some silent message shone in her eyes.

She's still alive.

A wave of relief washed through me until I realized what sort of life she must have. The guilt she must live with.

I didn't blame Rahanna, but I had no doubt she'd blame herself. I often still had nightmares to the soundtrack of her repeating *I'm sorry*.

I didn't know all the rules here yet, but I hoped I could talk to her again at some point.

Mr. Shaw continued leading me, oblivious, behind a tall hedge to a building with cream-stoned walls. Tucked away out of sight of the main estate, it appeared more functional than decorative, but was by no means ugly.

"This way." Mr. Shaw gestured toward a door. "These are the dorms for the conjurers. You'll live here. Inside, you'll find a place for you to sleep and keep your belongings."

I pushed the door open and stepped inside. I was about to ask for more directions, but the sound of the door slamming behind me was clearly the only instruction Mr. Shaw felt I needed.

Unlike the private suite I'd stayed in last night, this was more like a soldier's barracks. In the large open room stood rows of bunk beds—probably about forty of them. Everything was utilitarian. Gray. Spirit crushing. The space had minimal furniture and nothing of comfort.

People of all ages and genders milled around. A few gave me soft, sad smiles while the rest didn't react or didn't even seem to notice me. The feeling in the air was that of despair, frustration, and futility, not much different than how it often felt at the cotton-processing plant where I worked. Or used to work.

I looked around, searching for a bed I could claim. They were all the same with their gray blankets and white pillows. Each bunk had a small chest on either side, which I assumed were used to hold residents' possessions. Some beds were messy and unmade, clearly used, but I couldn't be sure the ones that were made didn't still belong to someone. I hovered at the entryway, unsure what to do.

"New arrival? This one's free." A young woman, about my age with tight black curls, waved me over.

"Thanks." I shuffled there, stood beside it and stared at the basic bedding. That was all I could do to claim the space. I didn't have any belongings to unpack. Mr. Shaw had taken my phone. I'd left my clothes behind in the other room and I doubted I'd be allowed them anyway. They'd probably been burned, considering the standards around here. I wished I had a printed photo of Nia to hold close, but the only pictures I had were on my phone.

"Since you're fresh meat, I'll give you the rundown. You get a bed, and you get a bedside to keep your uniform in. Bathrooms and laundry are down the hall, but you need to get in quick in the mornings if you want any chance of there being hot water. That big table down the end ..." She tilted her head and I followed the gesture to see a long table with bench seating, made of simple aluminum like what might be found in a park. "That's where food is served. You eat what they give you when they give it or you miss out. And you work your shifts you've been assigned in between. You'll most likely get a mundane job cleaning, cooking, or something like that."

Her words caught my attention. "Most likely?"

She leaned in, dropping her voice while she spoke. "They ship some conjurers off to other properties, but the unlucky ones end up at the sweatshops."

I gave her a look, urging her to explain further. Getting off this estate in any way sounded like a good thing.

"Don't look so keen," she scolded. "The factories they use conjurers at are the worst. You think being a servant here is bad, but that's where the bone-breaking slavery happens. We occasionally hear stories from servants sent there for punishment, forced to work non-stop until their bodies and magic are all used up."

I didn't have to ask her what she meant by that. Bodies gave up when worked too hard without time to rest and recharge. Magic couldn't be much different.

I was unsure of what else to say, but perhaps by being friendly, she might let me ask deeper questions. "My name is—"

"We don't do names here."

The meaning of that clicked immediately. Either they

didn't live long enough, or whoever supervised the conjurers made sure friendships weren't formed. It was standard practice on the streets. If someone didn't have a name, they couldn't be missed when they disappeared into the unknown.

I hadn't asked Ghost his name or who he was. Whether it was from habit or neglect while I had so much else going on, I didn't know. But the memory of him and his help burst into my mind then, as though it was jealous of more recent, more traumatic memories taking precedence. Had I really seen a ghost? I turned to the helpful woman, almost embarrassed to ask. "Have you heard anything about this place being … haunted?"

The woman scoffed. "You're worried about ghosts? You really are new. Trust me, kid, there's a lot worse here to be worried about."

I was going to ask more, but from the bed across the aisle, an older man stared intently at me. It drew my attention, and put my hackles up. Seconds crawled by while I tried to break eye contact with him. Something about him made my skin crawl, but I couldn't figure out what.

The moment I pulled my eyes from his, he spoke up. "I know you."

"I've never seen you before," I said with certainty.

"There's something so familiar about you," his raspy voice croaked. He must have been more than seventy. How long had he been stuck here?

The friendly woman stepped until she stood between us. "Just ignore him. This place makes all of us a bit crazy and desperate to find something, anything, to bring us an ounce of comfort."

I turned away, unsure there'd be anything I could draw comfort from in this place.

"I have to start my shift." The woman excused herself and left through the door I'd come in. I wasn't sure I'd ever call her a friend. She'd been helpful and I was grateful for that, but I couldn't trust anyone here.

I looked around at my fellow inmates. Most seemed broken and lost. Two girls clutched each other closer as they sat on a bed in the corner. Their similar facial features told me they were related, most likely sisters.

I was exhausted, physically and emotionally. I hadn't eaten since breakfast. That wasn't too unusual, but grief weighed heavier than my empty stomach. I flopped onto the bed. *Ouch.* It was hard.

I wouldn't sleep here—not in a room full of strangers. Over the years of homelessness, I'd perfected what some people called combat naps. Sleeping without fully giving up consciousness. It worked as a way to rest without making myself too vulnerable, so I could always be on guard for myself and Nia. Eventually I'd have to give up control to get real sleep, but I was so wired I couldn't yet even if I wanted to.

With nothing else to do, I lay on the bed, the image of the young girls clutching each other haunting me. I used to hold Nia like that when we were younger.

I had to find a way home. Our father wouldn't stop drinking to take care of Nia and she wasn't old enough to raise herself. I had to be there to protect her.

Darian's threats were clear. He used spellborns' families to keep them in line. It hadn't worked with Lainey because he'd already killed them. But he wouldn't hesitate to use Nia to punish me. Right now, the only way I could protect Nia was by staying here and playing along. At least the estate would send money to her and Pa, for my labor, for their silence. I just hoped there'd be some left after Sergio drank his share, and that Nia got a little bit of it for real food.

I dared a glance again at the old man. Had he ever tried to escape? Maybe he'd been trying all along. Maybe he'd been trying his whole life. How long have they been keeping spellborn as slaves here?

A shudder rippled over me. No. At some point, I'd find an opportunity to get free.

Maybe I'd see Ghost again, and he could help. The moment the idea formed, I dismissed it. I'd relied on him too much already, and I was still worried he'd somehow betray me, out my lie. Even that hanging over me felt like a debt—not that I

had a single thing of value to trade. If I asked for help from him again, what price would I be willing to pay?

Did it even matter? At this stage, I had no magic, no allies, and no way of getting out. Darian King had me beat.

EIGHT

AS THE ELEVATOR raised us toward Darian's grandiose office, I took slow, deep breaths to keep myself calm. But I felt like I was being taken to my execution.

After the test, he'd been disappointed at my lack of magic abilities, but that was what I'd hoped for, so I could just fade into the crowd after that. Why was I getting singled out again now? Had he found out I'd cheated?

I'd woken up this morning in the conjurer quarters, ready to simply get to work on whatever chores were given to me. I intended to keep my head down, become invisible, learn what I could about this place and plan my escape. Then Mr. Shaw showed up and told me Mr. King had summoned me. I'd tried asking him what for on the walk over, but it had been of no use. Mr. Shaw was a formidable opponent, and an obedient lap dog.

The door opened onto the vast space. The whole room had changed since I'd seen it the previous morning. New furniture was laid out in a similar spread to last time, but now, instead of featuring red accents, they showcased an aggressive wasp yellow. The changes weren't just in the furniture and decorations, but even in the tiling and wall panels. No construction could have been done that fast. He must have spellborn assigned to redecorate his office. Was it just chance I'd seen the change, or did this happen regularly? Everything was so lavish, so unnecessary, it blew my mind.

Darian sat at his shiny desk, his black suit now highlighted with a yellow tie—he really did dress to match his office. Despite the early hour, he had a glass of no doubt expensive alcohol already in his hand.

Mr. Shaw didn't have to announce us—the door shutting did that—and Darian kept us standing. We waited long minutes before he finally spoke. "Zani, I'm so glad you decided to join me today."

I didn't bother correcting my name, or the idea I had any choice in being there. I didn't want to do anything to draw his anger. Seeing him again brought back horrific flashbacks of Lainey's death. The man I'd thought gorgeous at first sight now appeared a cruel monster. Nothing about his features had changed, but seeing him a few feet away made me want to shrink until he couldn't look at me with those cold eyes.

Off to his side, just like before, was the hunched over man. He listed to one side while his similarly hard eyes glared at everything in the room.

I trembled where I stood, clasped my shaking hands behind my back, and did my best to appear calm.

Darian continued, any reply entirely unnecessary. "I've decided on the perfect job for you."

Dread welled up in my gut. I gave a simple nod.

"Given your pathetic lack of talent, I wanted to find a special position for you here at the estate, and I have the perfect thing." He paused, a smile beaming on his face. He'd said 'at this estate,' which I hoped was a good thing, but I knew how dangerous that smile was. The evil it hid.

"I introduce to you the only person more useless than you are—my brother, Peldin." His right arm swung out to one side, gesturing to the grumpy, scarred man who sat in a wheelchair next to his desk. So, it *was* his brother.

Darian's new form of rudeness managed to surprise me. To call his own—clearly disabled—brother useless in front of other people, while he was there to witness the insult … it was despicable. I loved my sister more than anything else in this world. But there was clearly no love between these two. Peldin's sour eyes burned with hate and anger when he

looked at Darian. I couldn't help but wonder what kind of person he was, given who he was related to.

Darian's bright white teeth bared in a predatory grin. "Zani, you'll now be responsible for Peldin's care. I'm so tired of seeing his hideous face, and I need someone I can trust to watch over him instead. I can trust you, can't I? I know you understand what having a sibling is like." Darian let his threatening words hang in the air like a noose.

A steam-train-sized shiver railroaded over me. I gulped and nodded. "Yes, sir."

"He needs general care, feeding, bathing—whatever it is the staff normally do for him when he's not skulking around over my shoulder. Those are all your tasks now, along with keeping him out of my way from now on. He's an embarrassment to me and the King name. It's bad enough everyone is out there gossiping about him."

I remembered the horrible impression of him the woman in the factory had done, and my heart hurt a little for Peldin.

Darian looked over to him and snarled. "But despite his uselessness, I have to keep him around, so you also have to make sure he doesn't harm anyone or himself."

My eyes darted over to Peldin. Was he violent? Suicidal? I wondered if Darian really did care for his brother, just a little, if he didn't want him harming himself. Maybe he wasn't entirely heartless.

Then he finished his thought. "We can't let him have the opportunity to off himself and further embarrass the family name."

Nope. Entirely heartless. I didn't risk saying anything that could prolong this tirade. Darian had humiliated his brother enough.

Darian turned his back on all of us and returned to his desk. He took a drink, then seemed surprised to look up and still see us there. He gave me an impatient wave, dismissing me.

I looked to Mr. Shaw, but he had already left. I hurried over to Peldin, grasping the back of his wheelchair to take him from the room.

A sharp slap on my hand made me jump. He'd reached back and swatted me away, then began laboriously turning the wheels himself. I followed along behind, too scared to say anything. I held the door for him, for which I received a hateful scowl.

Once the door to Darian's office was closed again, I offered Peldin an apology. For trying to take control over his wheelchair and self, and for everything that had just happened in the office. He ignored me, rolling on into the elevator. I didn't know where we were going, so I could only trail behind and wait beside him. He pushed the button for the next floor down with a gnarled knuckle.

With a soft *ding*, the elevator opened out into a hallway where dust had pooled along the edges. The meticulous cleaning that happened everywhere else on this estate clearly didn't extend to this floor. Peldin pushed his wheelchair out first and through the closest door.

Inside was a room laid out like a small apartment. The modest space had a living area with two cracked leather armchairs, a wooden desk covered in books, and a messy kitchenette with a cluttered two-seat dining table off to one side. Next to it was a door I assumed led to a bathroom, and on the other side of the room were two more doors. One was open, and through it I could see an unmade bed. Mobility rails had been attached to various walls with no regards to the previously elegant décor. They looked like new additions.

Peldin struggled to his feet as he muttered under his breath. Once standing, he shuffled over to the kitchenette, which was a mess of tumbled over bottles. *I thought Darian said other staff had been looking after him? This place is a mess.*

Peldin poured himself a vodka into a used glass. Maybe both brothers were alcoholics. I thought of Pa and how his problem had landed me here, and my lip twitched.

"I could ... make some morning tea, or coffee or ..." I offered. I had to at least attempt to take on my role here to keep out of danger. But part of me also really wanted to help.

"Just get out." He growled dully. "I can look after myself."

A CAGE OF GOLD AND LIES

I winced. This was going to be difficult, but I had to do what Darian told me to. I didn't want to risk angering him. But maybe I could risk angering Peldin. I straightened my shoulders and spoke softly but firmly. "I'm sure you can look after yourself." *Yet you're clearly choosing not to.* "But it's my job now, and if I don't do it …" My voice cut out; I was unwilling to put it into words.

Peldin dropped into the armchair. He closed his eyes and sipped the clear alcohol. "This is a new low. Even for him," he muttered, opening his eyes to stare into his glass. His gaze flickered to me for the briefest flash before going down to his drink again. "That should be me up there, in charge. This all should be mine—the estates, the businesses, and the money. Everything *he* has should have been mine."

His words sent an uneasy feeling through me. Peldin seemed as greedy as his brother. But he wasn't angry or yelling; he just seemed defeated. At least he was talking, and not telling me to get out anymore. I decided to treat him like I did Nia when she was venting. I listened, nodded along, and didn't try to offer solutions that seemed like I was trying to fix her. I moved over to the kitchenette and filled the sink to wash some dishes.

Peldin didn't object; he just took another swig from his glass. "I can't do anything. This sickness stole everything from me. Trapped me in this disgusting prison." He stared down at himself.

Prison was the word I'd use for this place, but it surprised me to hear it from Darian's own brother. Unless … An exhalation shot from my mouth. Had he meant *his body*? He certainly wasn't disgusting, but I had no idea how it felt for him, what the illness did to him, what pain he might be in.

I pried, trying to make some sense of my new charge. "You're not allowed to do what you want?"

"Why do you think you're being forced to babysit me?" His voice was so bitter, but also so disheartened.

I felt a sudden urge to try to cheer him up. I turned and wiped my soapy hands on my thighs. "Things aren't so bad. You've got a clean bed all to yourself. A secure roof over your head. Running water and power. That's more than a lot of people have. It's all worth being grateful for."

I cringed at the words as they were coming from my mouth. I had all those things now too, but I was still a slave. This was still a prison. Years back, before I'd found our single-room home, there had been nights on the street when I'd been too frightened to close my eyes, watching for any sign of danger while Nia slept. I'd go back to that in a heartbeat if I could be free and with Nia again.

"Are *you* grateful for being here?" He scowled, as though he already knew. "Don't coddle me. Don't lie to me. I know you've been stolen from your home. I know you hate this place, and you hate me."

"It's not you I hate," I offered.

He didn't respond, but his body slumped a little farther, as though the weight on his shoulders grew heavier. He closed his eyes again and the air in the room thickened with hopelessness. I stared at him as he sat there, eyes closed as though to shut out a reality he didn't agree with. It was obvious Peldin was an abused man. I'd seen the way Darian treated him. What would that do to someone's mind? I could just imagine the emotional scars.

Peldin's eyes snapped open, locking onto me as I stared. He let out a rough scoff. "You think I'm repulsive, don't you? I bet you find my brother attractive and you can't understand how we look so different."

"I don't. I wasn't—"

"It's not even real. Darian uses magic to look like that. Everything about him relies on the magic he steals. For a man not spellborn, he's managed to build his entire life on the magic of others, not caring what he destroys in the process."

Darian has no magic, like me? I found it hard to believe, with how powerful he was. But also easy at the same time. He simply forced others to conjure everything for him. He had an estate-full of spellborn slaves to exploit however he wanted.

Peldin drained the last of his glass and let it tumble out of his hand onto the floor, as though he wanted to smash it

but didn't have the energy. It thumped softly on the carpet. "If I was in charge … things would be very different."

"Different, how?"

Peldin closed his eyes again, then let out a grunt that told me this discussion was over. He huddled into the side of the armchair, his face still sour.

When I'd been given this job, I wasn't sure what the brother of Darian King would be like. I'd worried he'd be just as cruel as Darian. Maybe even part of me had hoped he could be an ally. But now it was clear.

He was just as much of a prisoner here as the rest of us.

Nine

IT WAS A long and awkward week. Most of my time was spent watching Peldin sulk. I tried to use the hours with him well, getting his space tidied and arranging with the kitchens to have proper meals brought for him, and myself, too, since we mostly ate together. We spoke a little, and he remained dull and bitter, although never angry or rude to me directly, which was probably as good as I could have expected. He never asked me to do anything for him, never instructed me in his care or ordered me around. I did what I could for him anyway, and did my best to treat him with respect and do nothing which might attract Darian's attention. It seemed to have been going well as I hadn't seen the monster of a man since he'd assigned me this task.

I had the freedom to move around the estate, but also couldn't leave Peldin unattended for any length of time if he really was a suicide risk, which I got the impression was true. More than once I caught Peldin staring at a handful of pills, a distant look on his face. Then he'd notice me watching and tip them back into the bottle, taking just one.

I slept in Peldin's quarters, in a small visitor's bed in the second room, which was otherwise filled with boxed up belongings. Not that I really slept. I dozed, partially alert all night in the strange place with a man I didn't know if I could trust. I would get up a few times each night and check he was okay, worried that if he was found dead one morning, I'd suffer the blame. The only time I was relieved each day was for half an hour when a conjurer came to take my place.

The first couple of days I tried to investigate the grounds, tried to find Rahanna again, tried to find out more about Ghost, or tried to find some way to get out of here. But the time was always too short. It was barely long enough to get back to the conjurer dorms, shower, wash my uniform, and join in one meal with the conjurers.

The food wasn't as good there as what I arranged to be brought for Peldin, but I was enjoying having any regular food, regardless of what it was. And it was nice to have some company other than him sometimes so I gave up searching and instead joined the others in my break. I'd hoped maybe they might know something that could help me, at least, but often they were just as disheartened and sour as Peldin.

When I walked into the room then to join them, I wondered if being there instead of continuing to search meant I had already given up.

No. I would never give up trying to get back to Nia. I didn't even know what I was without her. Every part of my life revolved around caring for my sister.

The woman who had showed me to a spare bunk waved me over and patted a spot next to her at the long dining table like she did every night. I slipped into the seat as a loud clatter announced the kitchen servants' arrival, pushing a large cart of dishes and two bain-maries. They opened lids and steam rose up as they scooped a little of each dish onto a plate, dumping them onto the table in front of the waiting conjurers.

My plate landed before me. On it was a thin piece of unnaturally colored fried meat, like the tinned stuff I sometimes got from the canned-food drives the neighborhood center ran. Next to that was about a tablespoon of grainy white mush. It wasn't a lot of food, and my stomach rumbled. Since eating more regularly again, my malnourished metabolism had come to life, bringing with it hunger pangs. Before, I'd been so used to going without meals I didn't feel it.

The creepy old man spluttered as he received his plate. "This is it? I haven't eaten since breakfast!"

"It's all there was left. Tomorrow is the next food delivery," one of the kitchen servants said. She shrugged apologetically in a worn down, it-is-what-it-is way. She served up the final plate and they left.

Most of the conjurers were eating already, avoiding the drama, but the old man stared at the plate like it was a straw on a camel's back. His eyes grew wet and glossy. "This won't fill my stomach, let alone keep away the hunger until next time I can eat. I can't live like this any longer."

From a few seats down, the younger of the two sisters I'd seen before made a sympathetic sound. I felt it in my heart, too. There was a moment in my life when I'd thought almost exactly the same thing as the man had just said, not long after Ma had left us. Pa had fallen into his booze and there was nothing for Nia and me. Sergio had laughed at me when I went pleading to him that I was hungry. That was the day I'd decided to leave school and start looking after myself and Nia, knowing he never would.

I wondered if there was anything I could do now to help the hungry people here. But even if I could smuggle some extra food out of Peldin's rooms, I couldn't fit enough in my pockets to feed everyone. And I sure couldn't magically make more food appear.

The woman beside me muttered through a sticky mouthful. "I served Mr. King dinner tonight. There was plenty of food available for him, and trust me when I say he would have killed me on the spot if his plate looked like this."

Grumbles of agreement ran up and down the table, but I also heard something else. Like a soft chant dancing through the room.

A flash of orange light exploded on every plate. When it cleared, there was a feast in its place. For a moment, I wondered if I had actually magically managed to make it appear with my thoughts. But someone else had spoken the words of this spell.

Food was piled high on my plate. There was fried chicken, a steaming bread roll, mac and cheese, roast vegetables, baked chips and more. The plate was so full, the edges disappeared under the meal so big I wouldn't be able to finish.

"What did you do?" A terrified shriek came from the older sister.

My heartbeat grew loud in my ears. I had yelled those same words at Nia.

The younger sister had a swelling grin of pride on her face, but it quickly dropped. "I just thought it would be nice for everyone ..."

Every person in the room had stilled, staring at them. Mr. Shaw had warned me it was against the rules to use any magic without authorization. Would he find out about this? Would someone dob them in? I glanced around in a panic

and knew no one would need to. There were security cameras everywhere on this estate, and there, up in the corner above us, was one, barely obscured.

The elder sister got to her feet, her eyes wild, clutching at her sister. "What are we going to do? We have to go. I can't let them take you. *Where can we go?*"

She stared about the room as though someone could answer her question. Faces turned away from her searching pleas.

What was the punishment for breaking this rule? It had her so freaked out, it had to be severe. But then I realized that wasn't the only problem. No conjurer should be able to do something like this. The younger sister had spoken spell words. She'd used a ritualist spell. They had been hiding her magical ability.

Light burst into the room again and the girl dropped back into her seat, clinging to her sister. Mr. Shaw materialized as the brightness faded, followed by two security goons. I gasped, recognizing the neo-Nazi one from when Rahanna was retrieved after her escape.

Mr. Shaw's face told us this transgression wouldn't go unpunished. "Who cast this?" He waved his hand at the feast. He snapped his fingers, and the man beside him whispered spell words. The food disappeared from every plate in an ashy puff. "If the offender doesn't give themselves up, I will have you all punished until they do."

A CAGE OF GOLD AND LIES

The older sister sat a little taller, blocking the view of the younger. Everyone else at the table glared at the sisters or looked down at the empty table in front of them. Mr. Shaw paced about and the energy in the room thickened until I was worried someone would turn the young girl in. Then what punishment would she receive? What would they do to her older sister to keep her in line? They were both so young.

"I did it." It slipped out before I could think through the consequences. The older sister's eyes softened as she looked at me, mouth gaping. She knew what I'd just volunteered for, even if I didn't. But I couldn't let them punish a girl so young, couldn't let these people tear those sisters apart like they had Nia and me.

The woman next to me edged away, as though she was worried she'd get caught up in my punishment. Mr. Shaw turned cold eyes to me and he strode forward. His hand landed on my shoulder before I could protest.

In a flash, we were in Darian's office. Except I didn't appear sitting in a chair, as I had just been. My legs gave out at the awkward angle, and I landed sprawled on my back.

"You again." Darian's voice was rough as he stalked toward me, staring me down as though I was a spot on the carpet. "I knew you lied about the extent of your abilities!"

"I didn't lie. I … I …" I stumbled over me words. I hadn't had any time to think this through, work out an explanation or excuse or plan before being dumped in front of Darian's fury. I scooted backward, trying to put distance between us.

"Then *how* did the food appear?" Darian spoke as though he thought I considered him an idiot, and that he was above falling for my blatant lies. He squatted next to me, his hand clamped on my neck and jaw, forcing me to look up at him while his thumb dug into my cheek.

Terror at what he might do landed on me hard. *What have I done?* I shouldn't have spoken up, but I hadn't been able to help myself. I kept seeing Nia at that table. Darian's goons pulling Nia out of her chair, then forcing her into a glass cube until Darian used her up. Her lifeless body lying on the floor just like Lainey's had.

But what if by trying to save those strangers, I was putting my sister at risk? What if, to punish me for admitting to casting unauthorized magic, Darian hurt Nia?

I panicked.

"Those sisters, it was them. It wasn't me." My admission burbled painfully off my lips, making my eyes and heart sting. I hated myself for letting fear get the better of me, but I had to survive, for Nia, at any expense.

But the look in Darian's wild eyes said it was too late. Even the truth couldn't save me now. "Trying to blame someone else? You're pathetic."

I squeaked, "It's true, I can't cast anything!"

A CAGE OF GOLD AND LIES

"No more lies!" His voice was so loud, I could have sworn glass rattled. "This has gone too far. I refuse to stand here letting you continue to make a fool of me. You've been lying to me since the day you arrived!"

The urge to fight back washed over me, but anything I said would make this worse. I didn't like his grip on me, or the intent expression on his face that sent a warning through me that this had become personal.

Darian's dangerously gorgeous face inched closer until his hot breath gusted onto me. He hissed softly, "You'll be tested again, and not only will you prove you're a ritualist, you'll leave me *amazed* by the results. You have until tomorrow morning, and if you tell me one more time that you can't use magic, that will be your last breath."

Darian stood and straightened his suit. Mr. Shaw grabbed me by the back of my shirt and dragged me to my feet. I wobbled there, trying not to vomit. *What am I going to do? He's going to kill me.*

A charming smile appeared on Darian's lips, as though he really believed he was right, that he could win me over with it, that every display of how disgusting he was inside could be washed away with that grin. "This is good news, Zani. Once you've proven yourself, I'll move you into the ritualist ranks." Before I could open my mouth to protest, he held a finger up in the air. "I reserve those spots for the most gifted. For those who are worthy of working with the king." He gestured to himself. This man had an ego unlike any other. I couldn't stand being around him; it made my skin crawl. "I can't understand why anyone wouldn't want such a prestigious position. So, don't think you can lie your way out of this like you did last time. One more trick, one more refusal to obey me, and I will destroy you."

He stared at me for a moment that felt like an eternity. My vision swam from the sheer panic racing through me. I had only ever wanted to protect Nia. It was all I knew how to do, and I'd gotten confused, messed up, trying to protect someone else too.

My stupid mouth had killed me.

Ten

MR. SHAW DRAGGED my senseless husk all the way to the testing rooms and locked me again into a glass cell, leaving me there alone.

I took some deep breaths, trying to calm myself enough to function.

The other two transparent cages were empty. I was the only one being tested tonight. Across the large space, a dull buzzer sounded and the heavy-security vault-style door swung open slowly. The creepy old conjurer shuffled out, looking dazed. He pushed a cleaning cart with dirty dishes on top of it and fabric laundry sacks on the lower shelf. Other cleaning equipment poked out of the sides like spines. Was that vault some kind of prison? Who on earth was Darian keeping in there? This whole estate was already a prison where he punished or killed anyone on a whim—why did he need a high-security area like that? If I made it out of this alive, I would have to ask the old man what was in there.

I moved in slow, careful motions over to the table where the testing objects had been last time, knowing I was being watched. I had to at least make a show of co-operating.

I groaned at what I saw. Instead of a range of objects and spells, there was only one option this time. And it was the most complicated spell from before. The bobbin of blue thread sat on the table, taunting me. The message was clear. There was one way for me to survive—to cast this spell.

I remembered Lainey smashing everything off her desk, rebellious to the bloody end. In some ways, I wished I could be like her and fight. But I'd also seen where it had gotten her. I had to be smart.

Who am I kidding? No amount of cleverness was getting me out of this. It had progressed too far. There was no way I could use the argument I didn't have magic again, because Darian wouldn't believe me no matter how many times I protested or failed these tests. And if he was a man of his word, he would kill me if I even uttered those words.

I needed help.

Last time, the ghost had performed the magic, not me—unless he was some kind of dissociative projection of myself that I'd imagined to explain magic skills I didn't believe I had. I almost laughed at the idea, but the thought that this place had broken me from reality was too scary. I hoped Ghost would appear not only to ask for his help, regardless of the cost, but also to have some company. Even if I was just talking to myself. I felt so alone.

As though the thought had summoned him, he appeared in the small cell before me.

"Hi." His gentle voice was the most comforting sound I'd heard all day. "Here we are again."

I hadn't expected him to appear so soon, if at all—I was still not entirely sure of reality anymore.

I positioned myself so the cameras wouldn't get a direct view of my face, picked up the spell sheet and pretended to read it as I spoke to Ghost. "Yeah, they're testing me again."

"I know. I saw." He hovered around me as the palest change in air color, a shimmer of light, with an occasional form to his face when he frowned or smiled.

I drew a sharp breath. "Have you been watching me?"

"Not, you know, all the time," he said hurriedly. "I've just been waiting for a chance to talk to you alone, so I could apologize, but you haven't been until now."

He paled, becoming almost completely invisible, and I worried he was going away. "What do you have to apologize for?"

His form shifted, as though he were lifting an arm, running a hand over his head. It was such a human gesture, at odds to his barely-there being. "That stupid riddle joke. I realized I was making light of what was clearly a very serious situation for you, and probably came across as insensitive. So, I'm sorry for that."

I gaped at him. In this world, where Darian King toyed with my whole life, here was this spirit being worried he'd been insensitive to me. "It's okay. And maybe if I wasn't so stressed I might have found it funny. You probably saved my life that night. And I didn't even introduce myself, or ask your name."

"You're Zari," he said.

The corner of my mouth twitched into the smallest of smiles. He must have found out when he'd been watching me, and he knew I wasn't *Zani*.

"And you are?" I asked.

A ripple ran over his entire body as though someone had skipped a pebble over him. "I don't know. I don't know who I am."

"Oh … you don't remember your life before?"

There was a faint shake to his head. "I remember everything that's happened since I became aware of myself in this form. When I think of what might have been before that, there's nothing. Sometimes I get a sense of familiarity, like with this building and a few of the people, but I can't remember why they're familiar."

I felt a pang in my chest for him. Did he have a family who loved him and who'd had to find a way to go on without him? How long had he been wandering around this estate, his soul mourning the loss of loved ones he couldn't remember?

A strange urge to hold him came over me. I wasn't a hugger, but it seemed both of us had an intense need for comfort. I folded my arms around my chest instead. "Well, when I've thought of you, I've been calling you Ghost. Is it okay if I call you that?"

He nodded slightly and tilted his head, floating closer. "You've thought about me?"

A blush of heat tickled my cheeks. I coughed. "It's the first time I've ever met a spirit, so you're kind of a standout event in my life."

"You seem to me like a person with a lot of standout moments. It was brave of you, what you did for the sisters."

I scoffed, puffing air at the sheet with the spell on it. "Brave or stupid? I just acted before I thought."

The ghost raised a hazy eyebrow. "And what did they give you in return for your help?"

"What? No. It wasn't like that." The words broke out of me before I could stop them.

"I thought people didn't do things for others out of the

kindness of their hearts alone." He turned my words from earlier on me. "So, what did you gain?"

I let out a long sigh as I worked out what to say to him. It was hard to put how I felt into words. I was angry, and scared, but under it all was a small sense of pride and strength. I'd helped the sisters, maybe saved them. But what did I get for that? The weight of my current situation returned, doubled down on my shoulders. My legs threatened to give out, so I slid down the wall until I could hug my legs to my chest.

Resting my chin on my knees, I looked up at Ghost. "I gained myself a one-way ticket to execution."

"You're going to be fine. I'll help you again, if it will keep you and your family safe." He floated down into a sitting position beside me and offered a soft smile on his transparent lips.

I sighed, knowing it was the only way to survive another day, but I still didn't trust being indebted to him. "How can I repay you? I have nothing."

"We're really still not past this? I thought we'd covered the concept of helping just because."

I fixed him with my most stubborn stare until he groaned.

"Fine, be that way. You can repay me by telling me about yourself. Tell me what makes Zari smile."

I gulped, gaped. Smile? What made me smile? Like it was trying to solve a riddle, my mind raced over answers and couldn't find anything.

"Wow, okay, that was not meant to be a stumper." Ghost sighed.

"I don't know the answer." My voice was tiny. "I can't think of the last time I truly felt happy. I don't know what I like. I don't know what I enjoy. My whole existence has been wrapped up in protecting my sister. I don't even know who I am beyond that."

Silence drew out for a long moment, the glass against my back cold and uncomfortable.

"I think it's obvious who you are," Ghost said. "You're a caring, loving sister, and a brave woman with a bright mind."

A tear spilled onto my cheek.

Ghost paled away to nothing then returned almost solid for a moment where I could make out the features on his face clearly for the first time. Playful lips, strong jaw, sad eyes. I wondered what color they once were.

The joyful tone returned to his voice. "All the other stuff, like finding out if you enjoy riding unicycles or painting artworks with cake frosting, can come later."

A wry chuckle escaped from me and I wiped away a second tear.

"You're still young. You've got your whole life ahead of you to find yourself."

I wished I could be as positive as him, but a lifetime of

danger and doubt warred inside me. "Do I, though? I'm stuck here in this prison as Darian's slave. But even if I was free of this place, the life I had—I didn't really have freedom. The poverty and responsibility were cages too."

I half expected him to tell me I could pull myself up from my bootstraps and go about living an amazing life, free to discover my higher self if I just tried harder. But he didn't. He nodded softly and moved a little closer. I expected the air to chill in his presence, but it warmed instead.

Butterflies erupted in my belly. Something about this man comforted me and left me wanting more from him. He seemed genuine about wanting to help because he was a good person, but I didn't know how to handle that.

I backed away from him and stood up. "I wasn't able to answer your question. I need to repay you some other way."

He gave an incredulous laugh. "What do you want me to ask for? Your firstborn child?" He drifted to his feet as well, and I watched for some expression to become clear on his ghostly face to see if he was serious. After several moments crawled by, he spoke again, and his face became playful. "Tough crowd tonight."

Just a joke then. I folded my arms as a sign I didn't think this was a time to be kidding around. He'd apologized for making jokes last time, but maybe he couldn't help himself. Part of me liked that about him. For a spirit, he was very spirited.

The good-humored expression on his face disappeared, and I desperately wanted to find a way to put it back. He asked, "You really want to repay me somehow?"

I nodded firmly.

"Then find out who I am."

"That's … that could be a bit more difficult than your other requests."

"You insisted I ask for some kind of payment. I'm a ghost, so what else should I ask for? Material objects mean nothing to me. The only thing I've ever wanted, or at least since I can remember, is to know who I am and how I came to haunt this place." His voice grew soft, almost too quiet to hear. "And maybe that knowledge will free me."

What he requested seemed like so little and yet so much. The one person I'd been able to ask didn't even know this estate was haunted. "I don't know if I can do that."

"Then maybe you could try and guess my name. That would be a start. Can you agree to that?" The transparent eyes staring into my soul showed his desperation to know who he was, and I wanted to know too.

"Okay, I'll do it." My agreement cemented the deal. Now I just had to survive this test. Then I could get to work at finding out who he was and removing my debt to him.

"All right then. What spell do you want me to cast this

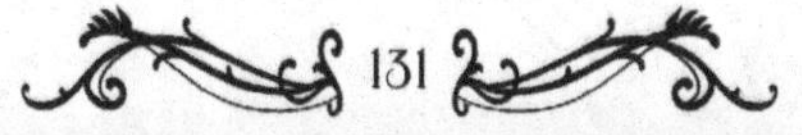

time?" His smile returned, though it looked sadder.

I had been thinking about what to do, and already had a plan. "They've only given me one option, but I want to give it a bit of a twist, if you can?"

I explained what I wanted from him, hoping I wasn't asking too much.

"Your wish is my command." He gave a slight bow with a smile beaming across his face.

I ignored his charm as it threatened to charge past the walls I kept around my emotions. I had enough to worry about with trying to protect myself and Nia. I didn't have room in my heart for someone else.

Ghost's energy changed and the room grew warm as he worked his magic. The blue thread on the bobbin brightened until it was a shiny gold, and it spun so fast, I couldn't make out the direction it was turning anymore. Something tickled my arm. A quick glance showed the thread quickly forming a finely knitted fabric encircling my waist and creating a smooth crisscross pattern.

I listened for the lyrical chant of the spell words to hum through my body, but there weren't any. Ghost didn't say a single word as he worked, despite the complicated pattern of the dress appearing on my body. A ruffled hemline dropped to the floor, then a fine mesh fabric like tulle formed larger, soft waves on top. After a few more seconds, the dress was complete.

A CAGE OF GOLD AND LIES

I wished I had a mirror to see the full beauty of the gown, instead of looking down at it on my own body. It was still majestic, until I noticed the drab gray uniform poking out from underneath. But I was also thankful the ghost hadn't removed my clothes as part of the spell.

I spun in a circle for him to admire his handiwork. I'd never imagined wearing a dress so incredible that it danced through the air when I spun.

"Absolutely stunning." The way Ghost said it made me feel bashful. There was a new light in his eyes, and he wasn't looking at the dress.

A small lump of sadness settled in my throat. I'd never known anyone as sweet as Ghost. I had to try to help him in return.

"Thank you, so much. For your help, the spell—everything." I lowered my gaze, suddenly too shy to look at him. "I'll do everything I can to find out your name."

"No, you won't. Don't endanger yourself on my behalf, okay? Promise me you'll be safe."

I stifled a sob that welled up from the mass of emotions this day had wrought. "When will I see you ag—?"

Ghost vanished.

An instant later, light flashed in green swirls, and Darian and Mr. Shaw appeared at the door to my glass prison.

My heart ached like it already missed Ghost. I wished I'd

had more time with him. I fought off the feeling and plastered what I hoped was an expression of meek obedience on my face.

"I knew she could do it," Darian declared.

I made my voice humble and apologetic. "I'm sorry I lied. I didn't know I was capable of this. I think I must be coming into ritualist powers, and it was the extra push you gave me that has awakened them. Thank you." I let the lie I'd practiced roll off my tongue. I hated the words, hated playing to his narcissism, but the stakes were higher this time.

"It's gold?" He leaned in to examine the dress, and I pulled back.

"You asked for something impressive, so I pushed my natural talent a little further. But like last time, if you touch the dress, it will revert back to normal thread." Darian thought I was hiding powerful magic from him, so I added something more to the display, to tie it back to my first trick with the golden bobbin, and give some consistency to my lies.

Before I could jump out of his reach, Darian's fingers grasped one of the wispy ruffles. The gold dulled into its original blue as the change rippled over the entire dress. Ghost had set it all up perfectly for me.

"Still at least partly useless then," Darian grunted, letting the blue ruffle drop from his fingers like a used tissue. "But you've proved yourself to be a ritualist, and are at least trying not to be a lying coward. I'm glad you've finally seen the light, Zari."

I couldn't hide my surprise at hearing my correct name. Had he been getting it wrong on purpose as some kind of sick power play?

He pointed a finger at me, his smile like a weapon. "You're going to be useful to me now, aren't you?"

I forced what I hoped was a polite curtsey. "Yes, sir."

When he turned and left, I felt as though I could finally breathe again.

I'd passed his test and survived another day.

But now Darian believed I was a ritualist. He thought I could cast spells and would expect me to do so at his command. And I still had no magic of my own.

Eleven

AFTER I PASSED the ritualist test, Mr. Shaw informed me I was required to move to their quarters. I didn't have any belongings to actually move, so I was simply taken there and assigned a room.

I looked over the tiny space. Although small, it was more private than the conjurer dorm, sharing with just one other ritualist. I had one half of the room, which was laid out like a mirror image on each side with a single bed, a simple wooden chair and desk. At the foot of each bed was a small chest which contained the navy-blue ritualist uniforms I had been instructed to put on ASAP. Whoever my roommate was, they weren't there right now but it was clear that half of the room had been claimed by someone, with a glass of water and pocket-sized ring binder beside the bed.

I had a binder on my desk and went to investigate. I flipped to the front and read the first page. "On the wall of the common area is a task calendar. Sign up for the tasks you'll be responsible for each week." The rest contained the approved spells I'd need for those tasks. I read over them, committing them to memory easily enough, but that didn't mean I could make them work.

I still had the blue gown Ghost had made me on over my other clothes. Which had gotten some odd looks along the way here. I guessed it was mine now. No one had asked for it back, Darian probably didn't have need for it, and it was designed to fit me. I took it off and folded it carefully for storage. As I changed into the new uniform, I thought about the conjurers I'd left behind. Would they miss me? Wonder where I'd gone or what had become of me? Would the sisters be okay? Would I get a chance to talk to the old man at any point now I was above their ranks?

I folded the gray uniform and wondered if I should return it. I wasn't a conjurer anymore—not that I ever really was. And I wasn't a ritualist either. I didn't feel right in either uniform. The navy-blue suit was fancier than the conjurer set. The shirt had a large hood which gave a theatrical air of magic to the wearer, and the ritualists I'd seen around all wore theirs up. I'd bet Darian thought that was funny, making us dress like his toy wizards.

I hovered in the room alone for a moment, wondering if Ghost was around, and hoping he might appear to me again while I was alone, but he didn't.

I stepped out of my room to explore the ritualists' common area. The furniture was also sparse out there, but still better than in the conjurer quarters. There was a dining area off to the left with an office-style break-room kitchen attached. There were a few older ritualists there, chatting between themselves. Was Cam around here somewhere? Was he still okay, still happy to be here? There was slightly more comfort and comradery here than there had been in the conjurer dorms. I wondered if the ritualists knew what their fellow spellborns' lives were like?

Down the hall, I found the shared bathrooms. At the very end was a sitting area with a few couches and armchairs.

On one of those couches sat Rahanna.

I wanted to rush to her, but stayed slow and casual as I sat on the same couch a few inches away.

She turned to look at me, frowning as she took me in. "Zari? Is it really you? I've missed you so much." Her arms slid around me for a brief moment. When she pulled back, she glanced around guiltily. We were no doubt under surveillance here too.

Her voice dropped to a whisper. "Why would you come

here? You saw what happened to me when I tried to escape."

"I didn't have a choice. They demanded *the daughter of Sergio*," I whispered pointedly, "come here. I've had to do everything they say, or they'd kill me."

"It would have been more merciful if they did."

Her words felt like a slap in the face. "Don't say that; you don't mean it."

"We die in every other way every time we use magic for him. Every spell we cast for him lets him keep hurting others." The wild, pleading look in her eyes told me she was on the verge of a freak-out. I didn't argue. The only reasons we were both still here, and not fighting to our last breath, were the lives we were trying to protect outside this place.

Several minutes of silence passed. I wanted to comfort her, but was worried about appearing too close to anyone, so I just leaned my shoulder so it barely touched hers. She sighed and leaned toward me too.

I didn't want to press her, but I was desperate. I needed more information and answers, and hoped she could give me some. I whispered, "When I first got here, I saw someone attack Darian."

Rahanna shot me a wide-eyed look.

"You know what happened, don't you? How the magic bounced off him and attacked her instead. How is that possible?"

"It's protection magic."

"But I heard Darian isn't spellborn."

"He's not." Her words were lifeless. "Every morning, he makes one of his most loyal ritualists cast a protection spell on him. It makes him untouchable, returning any attack back on his enemy threefold."

"How do you know all of that?"

A hard laugh escaped her lips. "Because I'm one of the ritualists who cast it."

I backed away from her along the couch. "Are you really loyal? To that monster?"

Rahanna's blank eyes met mine. "He's all powerful. If you love anything, anyone in your life, you'll do whatever he says. There's no way out. He has eyes and ears everywhere."

I thought about how quickly Mr. Shaw had come for us after Sergio had boasted at the bar. With Darian's resources, he could pay bounties for any hint of information on spellborn, or maybe he used magic to listen in? I felt completely out of my depth against someone so powerful. Who knew what his resources could achieve?

Rahanna didn't seem any better off. I barely recognized her anymore. This wasn't the best friend I'd met right after we came to Oramont. The Rahanna of my memory was full of life and rebellion. She'd do anything she wanted because she'd find a rush from it. That girl had lived on adrenaline.

This Rahanna … she'd lost her spirit. Her once warm skin was sallow, and her hair was limp. Seeing her like this, it made fear well up inside me. If I didn't escape soon, I could end up just as lost. "What has he done to you?"

"He broke me." She was silent for a moment before she continued, "Back on that day, there was a barely noticeable static in the magic barrier that fences us in. I only saw it because I was walking by when it happened. I thought it was luck … I reached my hand out, waiting to be pushed away, but there was a gap. As my fingers slipped through to the other side, I didn't stop to wonder what might happen. I just ran."

"That was the day I saw you in the alley?"

She nodded. "I can't believe I thought I had escaped. That I thought if I could get my family far enough away these people wouldn't be able to find me, wouldn't be able to hurt us. It was all just a test. A lesson. That Darian always wins."

A test? Then wouldn't Darian have set up the gap in the barrier so he'd know the moment she passed through and failed the test? Then a much darker, evil answer appeared.

He'd staged the whole thing. Darian wanted to flaunt his power any chance he got. If someone failed the test and left, they would be primed for punishment, for a fatal display of what defying Darian meant. When his goon squad showed up the moment she returned to her family, it wasn't convenient timing. It was to teach her a lesson by murdering a family member right in front of her. To give her the hope of escape, then crush her with it. It was cruel, but had clearly been effective in breaking her spirit. She'd known he wouldn't hesitate to order the murder of her mom or brother.

Rahanna wouldn't dare to break the rules again. She'd be one of his most loyal.

If I wanted to escape, the only way to really be free would be to somehow defeat Darian first. But I couldn't do that while he was protected by magic.

"Refuse. Refuse to cast the protection spell on him, so we can fight back."

She shook her head, pity in her eyes. "If one refuses, there will always be another who would do it instead, and the only outcome is we'd be punished. We all fear the consequences of disobedience. We're all broken."

I moved close to her again, sitting in silence, hoping I could bring her some comfort. Rahanna wouldn't be any help—not while Darian held her family's lives over her head, and I couldn't blame her. I wouldn't sacrifice my sister either. I looked over the hallways leading to the private rooms. How many of these spellborn were in the same situation? Could Darian really kill that many people? How much blood was already on his hands?

Darian had ruled over this estate for six years now. There was no telling how many he'd killed, and if his father had

been the same way …

"No wonder this place is haunted," I muttered.

"Haunted?" Rahanna asked.

"You've never seen a spirit here before?" I was surprised that with so many deaths there weren't more than one, but maybe ghosts weren't a common magical thing.

Rahanna half shrugged. "Not myself. There's an old conjurer who said he saw a ghost once. But I think his mind has been lost, scrambled from working the vault."

"I saw him coming out of there when I was getting tested. What do they keep in there?" *Or who?* "What do you mean scrambled?"

"There are spells of secrecy cast on anyone who works in that place, messes with their heads. Even the old man probably doesn't know what he does in there."

The poor man. I'd thought him creepy, but just like everyone here he suffered from Darian's cruelty.

My conversation with Rahanna was leaving me more hopeless than before. She'd been here for years and the only chance of escape she'd had was nothing more than a cruel lesson. *Am I ever going to see Nia again?*

As though she was thinking along similar lines, Rahanna asked with a crackled voice, "Have you seen my family recently? Are they okay?"

"I checked in on them when I could. Sammy's getting so

tall—you wouldn't believe it. Your mother … She's coping." I paused while gently grasping her hand. I went to her father's funeral too, but I didn't say so. It felt strange that I had been there for it when Rahanna hadn't been able to attend.

A ragged breath escaped from her as her hand grasped mine. She gave me a small nod, then stood to leave.

After taking a few steps, she turned back. "Zari? Don't make trouble, okay? It's not worth it. I don't want to lose you too."

TWELVE

DREAD BUILT IN me as I stared at the task calendar in the ritualist common area. How could I sign up for anything if I didn't have magic?

The ritualists had a lot more freedom to their schedule than the conjurers did, and during my first afternoon as one of their rank. People came and went freely at all hours, taking breaks and meals when they chose. The perks of the position didn't hide from me the truth that we were slaves though.

My roommate turned out to be a middle-aged woman with a pinched face and loud snore. She gave me the message the next morning that we would not become friends when she kicked my bed to wake me from my interrupted sleep and told me to go pick a job and pull my weight, or she'd report me.

Most of the tasks had already been claimed, but a lot of them required more than one ritualist working together, like the artwork creation and redecorations. Which did happen daily in Darian's office. I couldn't sign up for anything that would reveal my lack of magic to the ritualist I was meant to be helping. I looked for Rahanna's name, hoping to work with her, but she wasn't on the board. Neither was any mention of the protection spell or barrier spell maintenance tasks. They must be assigned elsewhere and limited to spellborn who'd passed Darian's twisted loyalty lessons. I saw Cam's name, but didn't know if I could trust him.

There was only one option available that was an individual task I had any chance of doing—a cleaning task. Maybe it wasn't taken because the other ritualists felt it was conjurer's work and beneath them. I signed myself on for it every day that week.

I had a quick breakfast while other ritualists came and went, taking a moment to stare at the new girl but not the time to offer a word of welcome. The most I was given was a pitying look. I headed out as early as I could with the small binder in my pocket. It didn't matter that I couldn't use the spells; I had to make everyone believe I could.

When I saw the size of the area I was meant to clean, I was worried I'd made a mistake. Without magic, the enormous atrium would take all day to get done. I had been hopeful yesterday, seeing how the ritualists had some free time, that I'd be able to explore the estate more, find out who Ghost could be.

My binder contained several spells that would clean the room for me, but since I had the magic ability of a rock, I needed to find real cleaning supplies. I'd seen the conjurers using some the first day here. Supplies had to be stored around here somewhere.

After peering into several closets, I found a small utility space several rooms over near the servants' entrance. Grabbing the duster, broom, rags, and spray bottle, I returned to the room and got to work.

I hoped Ghost would appear again, but although I worked alone, people came and went by so frequently he didn't show himself. The constant through traffic left my nerves frayed too, worried someone would question what I was doing. Every time I heard someone coming, I hid the cleaning supplies and pretended to cast a spell until they left. I also knew there were surveillance cameras everywhere, but after a while, I relaxed a little when no one appeared to question me. Maybe me choosing to clean by hand wasn't too strange, or against the rules, or perhaps I wasn't being watched that closely.

I had worked all day long with no breaks. It was late in the evening by the time I was done, and I was signed up for more again tomorrow.

I was grateful for each additional day I survived this place, but after a few days passed the same way, working my fingers to the bone and enduring snore-rattled nights, I was exhausted. And I hadn't found out a thing about Ghost, or gained any new insight on how to escape, or been able to see Rahanna again.

I was too tired to even feel rebellious anymore. My life felt like a never-ending cleaning session, and I leaned my head against the wall as I polished the glass beside me.

A nursery rhyme my mother used to say to Nia and me when we were young popped into my head. I often recited it when I missed her the most, or needed her strength. And I needed strength now.

"Guarded beloved, fair nursling sleep." I kept my voice low, singing the rhyme softly as she would. "Buss, buss, safeheart, no need to weep."

"Wow, what spell is that?"

I scrambled, trying to hide the cleaning rag in my folded arms, and kicking the window cleaner bottle behind my feet.

I turned to see a smiling blond face under a navy hood. "Cam? You almost gave me a heart attack!" Squeezing my arms around my chest, I willed the erratic beating to calm.

"Zari? I had no idea you'd made it as a ritualist! Congrats!" He raised a hand to high-five me, but I had the cleaning rag clutched in mine so I kept my arms folded. He rolled his

eyes but didn't seem too offended. "I haven't seen you since testing. How have you been?"

How could I sum up how I'd been, as though we were friends meeting on the street and I hadn't suffered the worst weeks of my life? I wasn't going to risk telling him the truth. I just wanted Cam to move on and leave me alone. I shrugged. "You know, okay, I guess."

"I've been great!" Cam said, despite my deliberate neglect in asking him. "I'm loving learning all the new spells. I just wish I had access to even more. I'm trying to prove myself so I can earn the barrier spell next. How about Lainey? Have you seen her since the test?"

My chest clenched again. I remembered the blood on the floor, the stillness of her gaze. The words of the spells that killed her echoed through my head. "She ... she didn't make it."

"Just a conjurer then?"

"No. She—"

Cam stepped closer and picked up the bottle of cleaner. "What do you have this for?"

I inhaled sharply. "Oh. You know, feel like I should do a bit of manual work sometimes. Just to keep active."

"You're kidding, right? Why aren't you using magic to finish this off? It's lunchtime already." He eyed me suspiciously. "I didn't see your name on the task calendar at all last week.

I assumed it was because you ended up being a conjurer, but now you're here. What's going on with you? You didn't trick them into thinking you're a ritualist when you aren't, did you?"

My blood turned to ice in my veins. My response lingered on my lips. I'd told Cam once I didn't have any magical ability, but if I stuck to that now, he'd want to know how I'd been placed into ritualist ranks. He could report me and they might find out I'd used the ghost's help. Everything could fall apart. "No, of course not. I just got sick last week and they let me have some time off."

"Suuuure." The word rolled out on a wave of sarcasm. "Show me then. Cast your proper cleaning spell and finish this up."

"I don't answer to you. Just let me do it how I want."

"Hmm." Cam muttered a spell and flicked his fingers at me. I braced myself for an attack, but none came. Instead, a flash of purple caught my attention. A glance at my hand showed my skin dimming from a bright violet into a dark blue, then brightening into a vivid green.

"What have you done? Cam, get this off me!"

"It's not going to hurt you. Pretty, don't you think? And you can remove it whenever you want. Just cast the restoration spell from the standard ritualist binder." With a smug smile on his face, he crossed his arms over his chest and waited.

I grunted in frustration, shaking my wrist as though I

could flick the colors away like water. If this didn't stop, if I was stuck like this, everyone would know I couldn't use magic. Darian would punish me for lying. He could hurt Nia, or worse, realize she was the real spellborn.

"Stop messing with me and get rid of this. You don't understand how dangerous this place is."

"This conspiracy rubbish again? Come on, this place is great!"

Fury growled through me. Without another second of hesitation, I stepped up to him, fisting the front of his shirt and pushing him back. A swoop of my foot took his out from beneath him and he fell sprawled on the ground. I dropped over him, pinning his arms under my thighs while I sat on his chest.

"What are—"

I jammed the cleaning rag over his mouth, forcing his jaw shut so he couldn't get out another spell. Then I leaned down and whispered into his ear, "Don't underestimate me. I've lived on the streets my entire life. I will do anything to protect myself."

Cam struggled, so I settled more of my weight on him. He looked around wildly, but we were alone, for now.

"I may not be spellborn, but I can still hurt you with my bare hands."

His hands opened, palms up while his entire body relaxed.

When I didn't let go of his mouth, he tried to nod.

"If you're trying to say that you believe me and will reverse this rainbow curse, blink three times."

Cam's eyes shut and opened once, twice, thrice.

"I'm going to let go of your mouth. If anything comes out but the restoration spell, you'll regret it." I pulled my hands from him while still keeping them close in case he made the wrong decision.

Slowly and clearly, he cast the spell.

I watched as my hand returned to normal. We eyed each other for a moment longer before I shifted off him, stood up and reached a hand down to him. He grabbed it, then straightened his uniform once he was on his feet.

I wasn't sure where that left us, and he seemed uncertain too, rubbing the back of his head and frowning at me, but also somehow still smiling. "So, you really don't have any magic then?"

I sighed and gave in to the truth. "Do you really think I want to do all of this by hand when I could mutter a few spells and then magic would do all the hard work for me? But no one can know. This place is worse than you realize. Cam, Lainey is dead."

That wiped the smile from his face. "What? How?"

"After the test, she tried to attack Darian."

Cam's shoulders dropped and he shook his head. "It's her

fault, then; she was in the wrong and got punished."

"No! Her brother, she—"

"You've had the wrong impression of this place from the start. You're thinking like a victim—not a winner." Cam's smug smile returned. "Look, I'm not sure how you passed the ritualist test without magic. But I won't pry … *if* you give me the spell you were muttering before."

My forehead wrinkled, trying to understand.

"The one when I first surprised you? Clearly you can't cast, so I don't know where you got it or why you were muttering it, but it's a spell I haven't learned yet and I want it."

The nursery rhyme? He had dirt on me now, and physical threats alone weren't going to be enough to keep him quiet in the long run, and I wasn't deluded enough to think he'd helped from the kindness of his heart. If I could get away with this payment, that was the best I could hope for. I just had to hope he didn't realize the words were meaningless.

"Okay then, but you can't tell anyone about my lack of magic, okay?"

Cam shrugged. "You're the one being the rule-breaker. But I don't actually want to get you into trouble. Your secret is safe. In return for the spell."

I repeated my mother's rhyme to him, feeling embarrassed, as though I were telling him the words to 'Little Miss Muffet.'

But he just took out his spell binder and wrote it down.

"Huh, is it like some kind of protection spell?"

"I don't know. Maybe?" I answered as honestly as I could. I'd always felt safer when Ma said it, but just having her nearby made me feel protected. I didn't think it was actually magic.

"Cool." Enthusiasm lit up his eyes as he wrote, and it gave me another idea.

"I have more spells I could teach you in return for help with my tasks."

"What kind of spells? I've already mastered all the basic ones in the spell binder."

"I know some others I've overheard. I only have to hear a spell once to remember it." I tapped my temple with my index finger. "I'm good with patterns like that."

"It's against the rules to cast unauthorized spells." The words came out more like a disclaimer than anything else. A couple of conjurers in gray walked past, and I knew I'd hooked Cam when he moved closer to me instead of away.

Once we were alone again, I said, "I'm guessing that rainbow nonsense was less than authorized. You're a bit of a rule-breaker yourself, aren't you?"

He raised an eyebrow. "Yeah, maybe. I like spells, okay?"

"How would you like the binding rope spell the security team use then?"

"Oh, yeah." Cam nodded. "Okay, it's a deal. I can help cover your little problem, and you give me any spells you manage to acquire."

We shook on it. Remembering the rhythm to Lainey's spell, I recited it for Cam as he took it down.

He nodded, then stepped away from me. "Can't wait to give this a proper try."

"When it's safe, of course," I snapped, worried that my deal with him would get him into trouble too.

"I'm not an idiot, Zari," he said.

Without me needing to ask, he cast the cleaning spells required to finish my task for the day. Seeing the room all cleaned and done with half the day still spare felt like a massive weight taken from me.

I thanked Cam, and he strode from the room without another word. After a few more minutes to return the cleaning supplies, I glanced around.

What would I do now? I should be working on finding out who Ghost was, or how to beat Darian, but I really just wanted to go back to my room and sleep.

Sleep in the ritualist dorm had been as broken as it was when I'd slept in Peldin's rooms, getting up to check on him through the night. It wasn't my responsibility anymore, but I felt a small pang of worry for him. He had been so sad and broken. In the time I took care of him, he'd never been overly friendly toward me, but he'd became less acerbic. There were moments with him I could almost say I enjoyed. Was anyone looking after him now, making sure he wasn't hurting himself?

The servants' staircase in the next room led to Peldin's apartment. It wouldn't take long to stop by for a quick visit and still get back to my quarters for an afternoon nap before my roommate started snoring.

I hurried over to the stairs and climbed them straight to Peldin's floor. When I got there, a bout of awkwardness almost turned me around, but I forced myself to knock on the door.

There was no reply. *He's probably somewhere else. Or asleep. Or doesn't want visitors.* The way he used to stare at a pile of pills in his hand popped into my worrying imagination.

I tried the handle. The door swung open, revealing Peldin reading a book in his armchair. He looked up at me, wide eyed.

"Sorry, I—" *Let anxiety get the best of me and thought you might have killed yourself in my absence? I'm an idiot.*

"Zari? What are you doing here?" He spoke softly, gesturing to the other armchair where an old woman in conjurer clothes slumped in a deep slumber. A mountain of dirty clothes towered in the corner and crumb-covered plates were stacked high on the coffee table. All this mess, and his supposed caregiver was having an afternoon nap? But Peldin didn't seem angry. He seemed more careful not to wake her.

Rolling from heel to toe while I stepped, I moved silently closer to Peldin so I could speak softly with him. "I thought I'd check in on you, make sure your new caregiver was doing a decent job."

"That's …" His sour and wrinkled face softened, almost happy. Then he grunted, "Entirely unnecessary."

I had to have imagined it. Peldin didn't smile, especially not to someone like me.

He grumbled, "It's been a week."

"It's the first bit of free time I had," I snapped back defensively.

His blue eyes shot to me, soft again, then away just as fast. Peldin closed his book, leaving his finger between the pages to mark his spot. "Darian didn't say a thing about where you'd gone. I thought maybe … but then I found out you're a ritualist now. So, congratulations, I guess. Moving up in the world."

"I didn't go because I wanted to."

He paused, and light danced in his usually blank eyes. His voice was a ragged whisper. "I know."

I squatted next to his chair. "Are you doing okay?" I gestured to the overflowing kitchenette and empty vodka bottles. In the week I'd spent with him, his drinking had slowed down a bit and I'd wondered if maybe he was feeling better. It gave me some misguided hope that back home Sergio could be getting better too, could be stepping up and taking responsibility and looking after Nia during the time I'd been gone. Seeing Peldin clearly turning back to alcohol made me sad. I wanted him to feel better. When had I started to care about what happened to him? Maybe I was just clinging to the need to care for someone when I couldn't care for Nia.

He grunted in reply to my question, then followed up with, "You shouldn't be here. If Darian sees you with me without permission, he'll punish you."

I frowned. Did Peldin care what happened to me, too? He was right though. Whatever free time I had, I still had to be careful. There was surveillance everywhere and it had been a miracle I hadn't been pulled up already with my manual cleaning efforts. Staying too long was a risk, but Peldin had lived here most or all of his life. I should take the opportunity while I could to find out more. Maybe he knew who Ghost was.

"Can I ask you a quick question? Then I'll leave."

He rubbed his arm while his eyes glanced away from me. "Ask."

"Have you ever seen a ghost in the Crystal Estate?"

Peldin's eyes shot back to me with his eyebrows raised. "A ghost? No, I've never seen one. Didn't think they existed."

Disappointment needled my eyes. If Peldin didn't know who the ghost was, how would I find out? "Well, do you know about anyone who has lost their life here?"

He gazed at me for a long time. His eyes were ice blue and watery, and his lips twisted. "Who hasn't lost their life here?"

I nodded slowly, and put my hand on his knee for a moment. "Thanks anyway. Try to have a good day. Look after yourself, okay?"

"Always do." He let out another grunt and resumed reading his book, but I saw his lips pull up again.

I moved silently to the staircase, then raced away. Frustrated and confused emotions formed hot tears in my eyes.

Maybe all our lives were already lost.

Thirteen

STANDING IN A quiet corner, I tried to stay out of view of the guests.

Darian's party was nothing less than extravagant. I didn't even know the occasion, if there was one or if it was 'just because'—just a way to flaunt his wealth. I laughed wryly on the inside at what Nia and I had once thought a fancy party was. I'd been way off. There was no ice-carved swan, but instead, magic had been used to decorate the space with thousands of lilies and roses made from non-melting ice. The whole floor glittered and shifted color, similar to the rainbow spell Cam had used on me. Every ritualist had been 'invited,' and we were spread throughout the room. But really, we were there to entertain the rich guests with illusions and spells. Although out of uniform, we were all marked by blue clothing in one form or another.

I stepped farther back until my dress squished between me and the wall. An hour ago, when I'd first put on the dress Ghost made for me, I'd thought it was the most gorgeous dress I'd ever seen, even though it was no longer golden. Glancing out into the swarm of rich party guests, I could see their looks of disdain, though I wasn't sure how much of that was because of the dress, or something else about my appearance. Or maybe it was because I was supposed to be spellborn—no more than a fancily dressed servant, in their eyes.

"Hate all of this too?" Peldin grumbled from beside me.

I turned and offered him a warm smile. As rude as he could be, he was one of the few people in this place I could talk to. "I didn't know you'd be here."

Peldin scowled. "Darian doesn't like me being around, but some of these guests are old family friends and it would raise more questions if I wasn't."

With a shake of my head, I took in Peldin. He sat crookedly in his wheelchair, one arm tucked awkwardly against his chest, wearing a neat black suit. It fit him well, bunching a little where he listed to one side. His expression was still mostly bitter, but he glanced toward me now and then, and his gaze was soft. It even looked like he'd washed and combed his hair. I'd thought it a mousy brown before, but it had nice golden highlights.

"So, we're both obliged to be here on pain of death, but maybe we can still have some fun anyway?" I attempted to sound bright and carefree.

Peldin didn't seem to enjoy my attempt at humor. Pain glimmered in his eyes before he turned away. Now I understood how Ghost felt trying to make me laugh. Maybe I'd completely forgotten how to be funny.

Peldin seemed to struggle to take in a deep breath that raised and rattled his whole chest, then he looked back up to meet my gaze. "I don't want—"

"Zari!" My ritualist roommate charged toward me and stopped just shy of us. She waved me over to her. "Get out here now!"

I glared at her and looked back to Peldin, to let him finish his thought. But he just glowered and gave me a shooing hand gesture.

"It was nice seeing you again," I told him, and hurried to join my fellow ritualist before she drew too much attention.

She poked a finger at my chest. "You're here to take requests from the party guests, not supervise Peldin," she warned in hushed tones. Her eyes narrowed on me, badly concealed fear on her face. "Darian is picky about how we act at these parties, and if you screw up, he's going to be in a bad mood all week. Now go do your job."

I couldn't blame her for having a go at me. She probably thought she was doing the right thing, keeping the trouble-maker in line. She was just trying to protect herself, too, and maybe others. We all knew how temperamental Darian could be. None of us wanted his wrath tonight, or anytime. It wasn't her fault she had no idea what situation I was really in.

I nodded and eased away into the crowd. I needed to get clear of her and find another good spot to hide, or maybe find Cam to help cover for me. Our deal had been working out well, and I still had one of Lainey's spells left I could trade with him.

An unguarded door came into view. Now all I had to do was sneak through it with no one noticing me.

"Hey, you!" a man's voice called out.

Pretending I didn't hear him, I kept on my trajectory. A hand gripped my arm and pulled me around. A man who was easily in his seventies, wearing a leather suit, grinned at me drunkenly. A woman a third his age, and three times as drunk, hung on his side.

"I said, 'Hey, you.' That means you." His tone was dangerous and teasing.

Plastering on the best fake smile I could, I addressed the man. "I'm sorry. There's so much noise in here. I didn't hear you."

He scrutinized me but didn't let go of my arm. "I want

you to show my wife your best trick."

This wasn't good. Frantically, I looked through the crowd for Cam—guests in suits and couture gowns trilled in amusement as ritualists floated them with magic or showered them in rainbow snowflakes. But no Cam.

"Can you still not hear me?" He raised his voice dramatically, like I was deaf and stupid. "Show us your best trick. I want you to impress my wife."

I had to rein in the urge to tell the man to impress her himself since she didn't seem interested in him. Her attention was on a young, attractive man off to the left.

I bowed my head. "I'm sorry, but you caught me at a bad time. I'm on my way to a bathroom break."

The man's fingers clenched tighter around my arm and his voice grew louder.

"Just hold it for a few minutes! You're here to please me. Now do some magic."

I flashed back to the bar with Sergio, the man demanding I do a spell for him. I grew angry. If I had any real magic, I'd turn this man into the toad he was. A streak of rebellion fired up in me and I snapped, "I'm not doing a thing for you!"

"What's going on here?" Darian's voice made my heart rate spike and my skin flush cold.

"Your entertainment is refusing to do her job," the man bit out before I could protest.

Darian turned on me, scowling as he took me in. "You? You haven't learned yet?"

"I'm sorry—"

"How dare you embarrass me at such an important event?"

Anything I could have finished my apology with was drowned out entirely under Darian's voice. The crowd nearby grew quiet.

"I've given you everything you never had, and this is how you treat me? I pulled you off the streets and gave you a real home, but no. All you homeless lot are the same—grateful for nothing. You have no respect for anything."

As his rant continued, anger built inside me, burning like a bonfire. Had he genuinely deluded himself into believing he was a savior?

A circle of guests formed around us, watching the drama unfold. They looked at me with such disdain—the ungrateful urchin, disrespecting the man who offered her so much. My upper lip twitched, and my hands tightened into fists.

Darian stopped for a moment, then chuckled. "Are you all seeing this? The dirty street rat is angry. At me!" There were a few mocking laughs from the crowd. Darian looked at me with a bright, dangerous spark in his eyes. "You want to lash out, don't you? You think I've done you wrong when I'm only trying to teach you. Very well then; let's have another lesson. Go ahead. Take your best shot." He turned his jaw toward me and waited, smiling.

Everyone at the party was watching now. Darian stood in front of me with his arms out innocently to his sides. "Come on. Hit me."

I shook my head, not trusting myself to open my mouth.

"You still don't get it. I own you. If I tell you to do something, you do it. 'No' isn't in your vocabulary anymore." He leaned in until his face was inches from mine. "Do it, or maybe I'll make a personal visit to your little sis—"

A crack sounded across the room. My arm had shot out, fury guiding it, slapping him across the cheek.

Or at least attempting to. Instead, my hand struck the magical barrier of his protection spell and pain burst across my own face.

The hit was much harder than I could have done alone, returning on me with three times the force. I stumbled back and barely caught my balance. Soreness radiated across half my face and my mouth bled. A whimper shot from my throat.

Darian laughed, and his guests joined in. "What was that weak little slap? Surely you can do better than that." His tone grew steely, cruel. "Do it again."

"Please, no …"

"Harder!" he commanded, a smug sneer on his perfect skin. "Remember what happens if you disobey."

I looked around the room for any help, any support.

From the guests, there was only delight in the drama. I was doing a trick for them, after all. From the other spellborn slaves, a mix of pity and anger, but no one dared to make a move on my behalf.

I wobbled forward and braced myself, hoping the pain wouldn't last too long. My body protested, trying to pull my blow, but if I held back, Darian would make me strike him again.

Gritting my teeth, I threw my fist into Darian's other cheek.

For a moment I saw only white, and then stars swam across my vision as agony bloomed through my skull. I flew off my feet, taking seconds to hit the ground. I fell badly, slamming my shoulder and twisting my back as I skidded along the floor. The collision forced all the air from my lungs and I was left gasping, unable to even scream in pain.

Was I going to die? Had I killed myself? The aching in my head encircled my whole existence. I knew only pain. A tear ran down my cheek and I couldn't gather the strength to wipe it away. My chest heaved as I tried to fill it with breath again, and my pounding head lolled to the side, dark hair spilling around me.

In the corner, I saw Peldin staring at me. His face was twisted beyond anything I'd ever witnessed before, wracked with obscene emotions. Silently, I begged for him to say something, anything—to stand up to Darian for me. He blinked sad eyes at me once, then turned away. Even he didn't move to help me or stop his brother. He faded into the dispersing crowd.

My heart ached. I couldn't trust him or anyone to help me.

Darian stood over me, spitting words my way then to some of his security team. My ears rang and I couldn't hear what he said, what my fate would be now.

Two beefy ritualists hooked their arms through mine and pulled me across the floor, my dress snagging and tearing along the way. When we reached the elevator, they let me stand, but didn't let go as they marched me all the way to Darian's office. I barely made it, my stomach sick from the pain pounding through me, and my legs wobbling.

One of the ritualists pushed me into a chair. "This is what you get for making trouble."

My hearing was still too muffled to tell if he was being sympathetic or threatening. I tensed to try and stay conscious as a wave of nausea swelled through me. Was my skull cracked? I must have had a concussion. Even if I survived the damage done, Darian was probably on his way up now to kill me anyway.

He arrived only moments later. The skin puffed up around my eye and I could barely open it. I looked at him, wavering, all senses dulled under the overwhelming pain.

"I have a job for you. To show your future commitment to me and remind you of your worth." He went over to the table with the decanter of brown liquid and poured some into one of the crystal glasses, as though this was any one of his normal meetings, then he strode back to me. "I have a problem with a business partner who is being less than helpful. I want to close this deal in a hurry, so I thought we'd add a bit of motivation for him."

I watched him, confused. My entire body shook as I waited for what he would say. Instead, he pressed a button on his gold-accented desk. Minutes ticked by in silence until the door opened. Two security guards dragged a body, with hands and ankles tied, into the room.

Nia? Sergio? My vision was hazed by pain and tears.

But as the body was moved in farther, it became clear. I didn't know this man. He appeared to be middle-aged, with bits of gray mixed into his brown beard and hair. He wore as fine a suit as any of the guests at the party had. A gag was stuffed in his mouth and his eyes were round with fear. The guards dumped him on the gold-threaded carpet and he lay there prone as they left.

What is happening? I blinked, and agony shot through my face. Nothing felt real except pain.

"This is the father of the man I'm making the deal with." Darian bent to look at me closely, examining the results of his protection spell as though appraising fine art. "Zani, one thing you will learn about me is I always get what I want. It's your job to kill this man as a message."

A message to his business partner or a message to me? No doubt both. Darian wanted me to feel all the weight of dealing out one of his punishments that could also be mine at any moment. I didn't want to hurt anyone, kill anyone on Darian's behalf. Maybe Rahanna was right. Maybe it would have been for the best if I'd already died.

"I'd stay for the show, but my guests are expecting me." Darian tipped the glass to his lips, sucking back the amber liquid until it was gone. Then he walked to the door, but stopped to glance back at me. "Remember what happens if you don't follow orders."

I stared blearily as Darian left me alone with his next victim. *My* victim. The gag in the man's mouth kept him quiet, and the look in his eyes said he'd resigned himself to this fate. My insides blazed. Every whimper of fear was burned out of me. I was no longer scared. I was furious. No one should have the power to strip the freedom and life from a person like Darian did.

I raised myself slowly to my feet, growling a feral cry which left the man sobbing. But it wasn't meant for him.

I turned every scrap of hurt inside me into steel determination.

I would defeat Darian King. I would crush him. I would prevent him from hurting anyone else.

But first, I bolted to a golden wastepaper basket and vomited.

I was still spluttering when the creak of a door made me spin toward the sound. Darian couldn't be back already?

Cam's face peered through the doorway instead. "Zari? I … wanted to check on you after what happened at the party. I heard you were up here." He took a step forward then paused as he looked me over. "Oh, man …"

I moved away from the stink of sick and waved him in.

He eased the door closed behind him. "You really shouldn't have riled Mr. King up like—" Cam hesitated again when his gaze landed on the trussed-up man on the carpet. "What's going on in here?"

"Darian didn't think his display of power at the party was enough of a lesson for me," I explained, gesturing to the man. "He's ordered me to kill this man for him, to punish one of his business partners for not making the deal he wants."

Cam's grin split wider, a breathy chuckle escaping before he read how serious my expression was. "What? Really? He wouldn't …"

The man on the ground moaned around his gag and nodded.

Cam put a hand through his blond hair, ruffling it into

a mess under his hood. "This … can't be real." He wrapped his arms around himself while he sat on a chair and shook his head. "The things that happen here … it's not how this training was supposed to go. I came to learn and practice magic, not be a slave. Not see things like *this* happen." He waved at my beat-up face and the man on the ground. "I thought I could ignore the bad parts—that they were just happening to people who deserved it. But this has all gone too far." Cam looked at me, his skin paled. He glanced around the ceiling, probably checking for cameras. "I shouldn't be here."

My eyes filled in sympathy for Cam. He was finally getting it. And that meant his life had just gotten infinitely harder.

Cam jumped back to his feet. "Don't ask me to help you do this task. I can't kill someone. Not for anyone."

I reached out and put my hand on his shoulder. "I wouldn't. I'm not going to kill this man. I'm going to save him."

The prisoner started crying, his head shaking.

Cam asked, "And how are you going to do that, Miss No Magic?"

"One way or another." I wasn't sure yet. I had an idea, but it relied on Ghost's assistance. And Cam's. "Will you help take this man out of here? I have one more spell I can pay you with. Just get him out and hidden, and I'll deal with the rest."

Cam frowned, his jaw working as though chewing through the decision. "You don't need to pay. I want to help. I think

I can get him out with some of the other guests. I have a couple of spells up my sleeve to get us clear through security up to the barrier. He's on his own from there."

I slumped in relief. If the man was at least safe, that was what mattered. Even if I couldn't work out the rest. I would go down fighting, and I would fight to the death. That way, Darian couldn't torture Nia to control me.

Cam helped the guy to his feet, and with a few muttered words, had the binds and gag off him. The prisoner looked at us both, awe and gratitude shining on his wet face.

"You've got to stay hidden, understand? No one can know you're still alive," I told him.

He gave me a wobbly nod.

"What are you going to do?" Cam tilted his head at me, frowning deeply. "Darian won't believe this man is dead if there's no evidence."

"Don't worry about it. I got this." I pushed at his shoulders, urging him to leave. He didn't protest, but shot me a long look as he and the man left the room. At the threshold, he called back, "I will take that spell after all. If we both survive this."

The door clicked shut, and I closed my eyes for a second, wishing with everything I had that the two of them would be safe, and that Ghost would show up to help me again now I was alone. How would I summon him? He'd appeared to me twice in the testing room, but I couldn't leave this office, and

Darian could be back at any moment. I also hadn't discovered his identity yet as payment for the last request. But Ghost had said he'd wanted to help me because it was the right thing to do, and now I had to count on that.

I opened my eyes and was going to call out for him but he was already there, a pale visage floating before my bruised face.

"Are you okay?" He reached a smokey hand to my cheek. A warm, tingling sensation spread through my face where his ghostly touch lingered. "He shouldn't have hurt you like that."

"You saw?" Hot tears stung my eyes. His kindness was more than I could handle on top of everything else, and I hated that Ghost had seen me beaten and humiliated.

The ghost pulled his hand back and nodded. "Yes. I was there, watching, useless and invisible. I wanted to help, but … I can't use my magic unless I make myself more substantial. Being like this—it takes a lot of effort."

I hadn't known revealing himself to me was hard for him. And I understood why he only wanted to when we were alone. "It's okay. But I do need your help again now." An apology was on my lips, but I held it back.

He nodded. "I can heal you."

"You can't. Thank you, but I don't have access to healing spells, so if I'm healed it will only raise more questions."

Ghost shifted closer, so close I felt like I could breathe

him in. "I can at least make sure there's no internal damage though. Let me at least do that for you. I can't stand seeing you so hurt."

A tear dropped from my eye as I nodded my permission. I'd barely straightened my head again when a warmth swirled through me, sparking and tingling along my cheekbones, swarming the most painful parts of my skull. My thoughts grew clearer. The nausea was gone. My face still ached terribly, but inside, I felt repaired.

Air rushed from my lungs in relief. "Thank you."

Ghost lowered his face near mine, just one corner of his mouth visible, turned upward. "Anytime. But you were going to ask for something else?"

"Yeah. I actually need a different favor. Did you see the man here before, that Darian ordered me to kill?"

"I did."

"Good. That makes it a little easier. I had a friend help him to safety, but Darian will punish me if there's no evidence that I did what he asked." I explained to Ghost want I wanted him to do for me, and then I couldn't hold back my apology any longer. "I'm sorry. I still don't know who you are. I haven't got anything to pay you with."

"Well, I guess I'll just leave then," Ghost muttered.

A soft squeak came out of my wide-open mouth.

"Oh, come on. I'm kidding! I'm going to help you. Of

course, I'm going to help you." His tone was so tender it made me shiver. "I only wish I could do more for you."

"You've done so much."

Ghost smiled and a bright, golden light flared through the room. When it receded, a perfect statue depiction of Darian's victim stood against the wall of the office. Just like last time, Ghost hadn't uttered a single word, let alone a spell. The statue was polished gold, matching the current color scheme of the office.

When Ghost was done, he glanced around the room then looked to the ceilings as Cam had. "There are no cameras in here, but I'll make sure the man and your friend aren't spotted on their way out. Sorry I haven't been able to reveal myself enough to help you cast your daily tasks. But I've been doing my best to keep you covered on the security camera side."

Was that why none of my weird behavior had been called out so far? Ghost had been looking out for me and doing something to the camera feeds. I had no idea he'd be able to do that. Just how powerful was he?

My heart swelled with gratitude and before I could rethink it, I stepped forward and wrapped my arms around the space he occupied. My body sunk into the air. There was only the barest hint of warmth to prove I was touching anything at all. "Thank you."

The elevator dinged.

I drew away from Ghost and his form rippled, vanishing before my eyes. "Be careful, Zari."

The moment I couldn't make out his form anymore, Darian threw the door open. On a deep breath, I pushed down my ragged emotions. Between Cam and the ghost helping me, and Darian's blackmail, my feelings were all over the place. I hoped Cam made it. I hoped this trick would work. Forcing my stinging lips to curl into a smile, I greeted Darian with an expression of utter obedience and humility.

"It's done." I gestured toward Ghost's golden statue. "I know you like unique decoration pieces. And I didn't want to make a mess, so I made the man into a statue of pure gold for you, as a reminder of your power." The words ripped at my heart as I forced them out.

Darian's shining, white-toothed grin returned. "You surprise me. What a wonderful idea. How were you able to create such a thing?" He leaned in close, examining the features of the statue. When his finger reached out, I made a squeaking noise.

"Just my normal magic, but like all my magic, if you or anyone else touch him, it will revert back. The man will return, and you'll lose this fine new feature for your office."

Darian's hand hovered for a moment, then withdrew. He looked the statue up and down, then nodded. "I'm pleased. Maybe I'll have you turn all those who oppose me to gold.

What a collection I could have."

I shivered, unable to contain my disgust. "Yes, sir."

I was dismissed with the flick of his wrist—just a simple transaction completed, in his mind. As I walked away, my smile grew, stretching my aching cheeks.

This was a small victory. Darian tricked. One life saved. But it had given me hope again.

FOURTEEN

I SLEPT HEAVILY that night, the first solid sleep I'd had in weeks. Even my roommate's snoring fell on deaf ears.

It was early when I woke, and saw a note slipped under the door addressed to me. It said Darian had summoned me before I started my daily tasks. I stared at it blearily for a moment, unable to rouse any strong emotion. I should be scared in case he'd worked out we'd tricked him out of a victim, but a hardness had grown inside me, rebelling against the very idea of fear.

I was still in my ball gown, having returned straight from Darian's office the night before and collapsed into bed. I changed quickly, then headed straight to see him again, ready for whatever he'd throw at me next.

Rather than taking the elevator, I emerged from the servants' stairs into Darian's office, then stopped mid-step. A ritualist stood there beside Darian in the middle of the room, chanting the same spell over and over. Her voice was familiar.

"Hand or heart, bodkin or bane,

Naught will fret, thine foe be lost.

By circumjacent shield fane,

Cannonade thrice in power riposte."

Was that the protection spell? Worried I was too early, I made to back out of the room, but Darian's voice stopped me.

"Zani! I wanted to tell you, I'm quite impressed with your talent. This statue is exactly what I didn't know I needed."

I saw with relief it was still standing there against the wall. The ritualist continued chanting as though there had been no interruption. The figure's head was bowed low, the hood covering their identity. Maybe Darian didn't want to look his slaves who cast his protection spell in the eye. The ritualist finished, bowed, and headed toward the stairs. It was Rahanna. She glanced at me and then turned away, shame in her eyes.

Darian returned to his desk, which was still gold, as it had been the day before. "Since I'm a generous man, I thought I would reward you with a gift of my own." He didn't wait for me to acknowledge what he said before he continued. "Between the drama at the party, and your elegant handling of my business problem, I think you've learned your lesson. Because I'm such a great guy, and want everyone taken care of, you can have today off from your tasks while you heal."

Because he was such a great guy? I wanted to kick him, but already knew how that would turn out. How deluded was this man? He had to be fully committed to his narcissistic fantasy to think he was giving me a gift after what he'd made me do.

But if he really thought he was helping out, maybe he would give me a healing spell. I wouldn't be able to use it, but I could trade it with Cam so he could heal me. "Do you mean I will be granted access to the healing spells?"

Darian laughed heartily. "No, no. I think your healing should be slow, so you have the time for the lesson to really sink in. Best for everyone that you don't forget your mistake too soon. You're dismissed."

Darian turned his back to me without a care in the world. He knew I couldn't hurt him—not with that protection spell in place. Frustrated, yet determined to not mess up this reprieve, I returned to the ritualist dorm.

I thought about Ghost the entire walk back. He'd done what I requested even though I didn't know his name yet. He'd been helping me in other ways as well, without even being asked. When his hand touched my cheek, he'd looked genuinely concerned.

I couldn't remember the last time anyone had cared for

me, looked after my needs. Ghost wasn't only trying to keep me alive, either. He wondered what made me happy, tried to cheer me up with jokes. Was Ghost just being that thing I wasn't sure I believed in—a good and kind person—or was it something *more?*

My chest felt full, spilling heat up my neck. I was being silly, thinking of Ghost in that way. I was just having these feelings because he was the first entity to be kind to me in years.

I protected and cared for Nia because she was my sister, because I loved her, and I'd avoided other relationships for a reason. The concept of love felt complicated to me. In some ways, it felt like a binding, a responsibility, a debt.

But it also felt like … warmth.

I turned on the spot, wondering if Ghost was nearby, invisible and watching. I didn't want to be in debt to him. I wanted to give him something in return. I had the day off and would use it to try to discover who Ghost was.

The minute I entered the common area, Cam jogged over and dragged me to a free couch in the farthest corner of the room.

"I can't believe you pulled it off!" He spoke low, despite no one else being nearby. "I got the guy to the exit and he got out with the other guests. I was sure we were all going to be busted! How did you do it?"

"It's complicated." I exhaled slowly, thinking it through.

A CAGE OF GOLD AND LIES

I pulled my hood down and worked at braiding my undone hair while deciding if I could trust Cam. I didn't like the idea of trusting anyone, but he'd risked his life, and possibly his family's, for me and a man we'd never met. I felt like I owed him an answer. "There's a ghost here at the estate. He's been helping me."

I half expected Cam to laugh, but he just slapped his hand on my knee. "What? No way!"

"Have you seen him too?" I hissed.

"No, I didn't even know ghosts existed, but I've learned to trust what you're saying these days."

"Oh." I deflated. Clearly, Cam didn't know anything helpful.

"A ghost, huh? What's he like?"

"He's … really nice." Oh man, I was blushing. I pulled my hood back up again and cleared my throat. "I've been trying to work out who he is. He can't remember his name, his life—anything."

Cam huffed. "This place is old. It could be a lot of people."

"I get the impression he hasn't been around for long. Who has died here recently?"

"Allister? He was the most powerful ritualist at this estate." Cam smiled sadly. "I was so excited to learn from him, but he died not long before we arrived."

Another idea struck me. "What about Lainey's brother …

Ethan? She told me about him. Darian killed him, probably not long before we arrived too."

Cam leaned forward on the couch and rubbed his face. "I didn't know. I have two kid brothers, you know, out there."

"I have a sister," I said softly.

Cam nodded, his jaw clenched.

A darker thought popped into my mind. "Did Ronald King live here when he died?" If Darian had done something to speed up the process of his inheritance, that could definitely leave unfinished business. From what I could remember, it was about six or seven years back, which might fit Ghost.

"Based on the gossip about what happened, yeah, he died on this property. But the inheritance was Peldin's not Darian's, so I'm not sure there was a conspiracy there. Darian only took over when Peldin got sick."

I bit my lip, thinking it through. Peldin did seem really bitter about being denied his inheritance. I didn't want to believe he'd kill his own father, but I couldn't discount it with what I knew about the King family. That gave me three names to start with: Allister, Ethan, and Ronald.

Cam had been staring at my face as I sat silently with my thoughts. "How are you feeling?" he asked softly.

I winced. The swelling had eased a little, but the bruises throbbed, giving me a permanent headache. "Who knew I had such a good right hook?"

Cam snorted.

"Hey, you want that spell I promised you?"

Cam grinned and nodded, and I repeated to him Lainey's final spell—the one that had caused so much blood, then caused her death. "It's a deadly one, so be careful. And you can't tell anyone about Ghost."

"Sure, no problem." He gripped my hand briefly and squeezed it before standing up. "Stay out of trouble, okay?"

I nodded, knowing it was exactly what I wasn't planning on.

I left the common room to wander the estate grounds. As I walked through the immaculately trimmed hedge rows and magically blooming rose gardens, I thought about my next steps. I trusted Ghost to help me, but I couldn't go on like this. I wanted to repay him for his kindness, but what if I never found out his identity? At the end of the day, it was up to me to find a way off this estate and get back to Nia, no matter what. Even if we had to flee the city, Darian couldn't hunt us forever. Eventually, he'd give up ... wouldn't he?

I trailed around the outer-most edges of the estate, getting a feel for the magical barrier wall. Reaching out to it made me uncomfortable, and the hair stood up on my arm. I walked for hours in both directions looking for any sign of weakness, but I couldn't find a thing. Based on Rahanna's story, I wasn't sure I could trust an opportunity to escape even if I did find one.

But I would keep checking when I could. At least if I did find something, I'd have the advantage of suspecting it was a trap. I could work out some way to beat it. But there was nothing today.

Resigned to spending another night in this prison, I went back to my room and flopped onto the bed. The pain in my head had faded but was still enough to leave me woozy. I wished I at least had an aspirin. I closed my eyes, hoping to get some sleep in before my roommate returned.

A knock at the door disrupted my napping efforts. I wondered for a moment why my roommate was bothering to knock, but when I opened the door, Peldin was there.

"I don't want to bother you, but I … needed to apologize." His rough voice sounded softer today, and he seemed even smaller in his wheelchair than usual. "At the party, I wanted to help you. I *wanted* to. But there was nothing I could do."

The humiliation of the night before returned like a slap. There wasn't *nothing*. He could have said something. Spoken out. He could have rallied the spellborn to him like an army and burned this whole place to rubble to stop his monster brother. Uncontrollable rage built in me, followed by a tide of quelling truth. None of that could have happened. Everyone had stood and watched me take a beating at Darian's orders because it kept them alive, and it kept their loved ones alive, and I didn't blame a single one of them.

"It's okay," I murmured.

"It's not okay!" His hand smacked down on the arm of his wheelchair, and a sharp clap pierced the corridor. A ritualist scuttled past, pretending they weren't seeing or hearing anything.

"Nothing about what Darian is doing is right." Peldin sighed, slumping farther to the side. His features were twisted and anguished. "If I wasn't like this, I could stop him. If I wasn't … broken. I hardly remember what it was like to be healthy. I don't even have the strength to get out of bed most days. I can't do anything to stop this."

I wanted to tell him it was okay, that it wasn't his burden alone, that everything would work out, but it all felt insincere. He was opening up to me in a way he never had before, and my heart broke for him. "Is there anything I can do for you? Anything more that could be done medically, or magically, to make you feel better?"

Peldin glowered furiously. "This isn't about me! I'm already lost. This is about you. *You*. I want you to be safe. Unhurt. Free. I don't want *him* to hurt you. You're one of the few people who has been kind to me, since my body has been like this, and I wish I could do something in return. But I'm useless. Worthless."

"You're not! Not in any way." I knelt beside his chair so I could force him to make eye contact with me. When he did, there was so much despair in his ice-blue eyes.

I wanted to know more about him, what had brought him to this point. His face was worn and warped from his illness, and I wished he didn't have to suffer like this. Cam had said Peldin should have been in charge of all the Kings' affairs and wealth instead of Darian, and I could only imagine how different things would be if he were. Beneath Peldin's bitterness there was definite kindness. He never forced his caregivers to do anything for him, never treated me like a servant.

But there was nothing he could do against Darian physically. None of us could. With Darian's influence and power, I doubted there was anything Peldin could do legally either. In his situation, I could imagine feeling useless too.

I reached out and took his hand in mine. It was thin, and bony. He looked at me, pale eyes highlighted by a wet sheen. His hand shook in mine and he snatched it back, turning away.

"I'm sorry. I'm so sorry," he grumbled, and pushed his wheelchair off forcefully, speeding out of the dorms.

My heart hurt for Peldin. And there was some other emotion growing there beside that ache, something softer. I buried it away.

I couldn't let myself be distracted with pity for others. If I was going to survive this and get back to Nia, I had to look out for me and me alone.

FIFTEEN

PELDIN HAD LEFT hours ago, but I still couldn't seem to rein in my seething rage at how Darian had destroyed his life. Or mine.

I paced like a caged beast, sobbing and growling.

My roommate came by, took one look at me, and left again without a word.

I kicked the back of the door. I wanted to trash the room, but there wasn't enough in there to be worth it. I flung my spell binder at the wall. Unsatisfying. After tearing the covers off the bed, I dropped myself onto the mattress, squeezing my hair in my fists and sobbing.

I missed my stupid, horrible life outside this place. I missed Nia. Trapped here on this estate, I couldn't even be sure Nia was living free like Darian had promised. How would I know if his men had taken her unless he told me? How did I know she was even still alive?

I rolled over on the bed, then sucked in a gasp of air.

Ghost was in my room. He hovered awkwardly beside my bed. "Sorry, I didn't know if you wanted to be alone, or you needed somebody … not that I have one, but you know."

"Have one what?" I blinked away enough tears to see more clearly.

"A body."

I snorted an ugly, wet laugh, and chased it with a sob. I tried to wipe the saltwater and emotions off my face. "Ugh, I'm a mess."

"You don't need to clean up on my account. You've been through a lot. Feel what you need to feel." The tenderness in his tone made my breath shiver from me.

"I need to feel free," I whispered the admission. "But Darian would rather I died first."

Ghost blew a raspberry. "We can't have that. You're my only friend."

Friends? Was that what we were? His words made a sensation I couldn't name settle deep in my chest. "I never really had many friends either. Rahanna was my best friend for a while, until she ended up here."

"But you had a sister too?"

"I *have* a sister," I snarled at him.

He backed away, faded almost from sight.

"I'm sorry," I cried softly. "I'm sorry I snapped at you. I just miss her so much, and I'm so scared of something happening to her. Or that maybe something already has."

Ghost returned more clearly again, and I could see the shape of his face, the concern around his eyes. "What if you could visit her? Would that help?"

Hope popped me into sitting upright in a flash. "You could do that?"

"Not physically, but I think I could pull your spirit out of your body for a short time. You'd be able to see your sister briefly. I would do that for you."

I searched his face for any emotion I could find. Why would he continue to help me? Magic of that level couldn't be easy. "And you don't want anything in return?"

"Wow. She's finally starting to get it." He leaned forward, a wide grin floating on his face.

I smiled bashfully in return. Although he didn't ask, I still wanted to repay him. "I have a few ideas for who you could be. Nothing I'm sure about—just a few names."

Ghost drifted in the air silently for a moment. "Tell me when you get back. Just in case."

Just in case I'm right, and he vanishes forever? I'd wondered the same thing, but the thought that he considered

it a possibility too made me feel like I was already grieving his absence.

Ghost clapped his hands silently. "Now, let's get your spirit out of that body so you can see your sister."

I wanted to ask him if he was sure, but before I could open my mouth, a deep chill ripped through me for a second, then I felt nothing. I heard a thump and turned around. I looked back to see my body laying at an awkward angle on the bed. I held my hands up to my face and they had the same hazy appearance as Ghost's.

He'd done it.

"Go on, check on your family. I can't keep you like this for long."

"How?" I panicked, unsure how any of this worked, whether I could even get off the estate in this form.

"You're from the warehouse district, right?" A smile spread across his face. "I'll give you a push."

My surroundings blurred, sling-shotting past my vision. The grounds of the estate flashed by; the boundary of the magical barrier disappeared behind me. *I made it past.* I flew over the sparkling city skyline. Within seconds, I was down on a street in Oramont. It was late, and the sidewalks were bare of anyone who could potentially observe me haunting them. I giggled at the thought, and turned to get my bearings. I was only a couple of blocks from home. I tested my limbs, tried a step. I could move as my body normally would, although I glided much faster without the physical world holding me back.

I jumped off the dirty concrete and floated like a cloud up to the rundown room my family called home. I didn't need to open the window; I faded right through it. My heart backflipped at the sudden worry that Nia wouldn't be there, but the second I was inside there was an unmistakable cry.

"Zari?" Nia sat up on the bed, partially lit by the streetlights leaking through the torn film of newspaper on the window.

"Nia, I've missed you so much!" I flung myself at her and wrapped my arms around her, but they passed right through her body. I almost tumbled down to the floor beneath before I got my spectral form under control.

"What happened to you?" Her voice cracked. "Are you dead?"

"No! No, I'm okay. This is a spell. This was the only way to see you since Darian doesn't let us leave the estate."

Her eyes grew wide as she waved a hand through my body. "Do you know magic now?"

I shook my head and thought about Ghost. "A friend did this for me." I perched on the edge of our shared mattress, like I had so many times in the past. "I only have a little time, so tell me highlights of what's happened since I left."

Nia grew quiet as she looked down at the same rag doll she'd shown her magic to me with. "We get the money they said we would, but Pa drinks most of it away."

I looked over the space, making note of some packets of food, some new clothes, confirming what she'd said. At least Darian had held up that end of the bargain.

Sergio lay hanging off his mattress, in a slumber so deep he didn't twitch or moan like he often used to. He only slept silently when he was blackout drunk. Anger rose in me at his inability to act like a caring parent.

Nia saw me looking. "I guess that's not technically a highlight though, is it?"

I laughed softly. *Calm down, Zari. You're here to see Nia—not to waste the time being angry at Sergio.* "How are you holding up? You managing with school?"

Her lips grew into thin, tight lines, but she nodded. "I go to school, run the errands, do the chores, and fight with Pa about money. He knows I hide it in places like you used to. Sometimes he finds a cash stash, but not all of them."

"Don't give in to him. You need that money. Save it up; get yourself some fake documents like I wanted to for you. You'll be okay." I wished I was right.

Nia nodded, then left her head hanging with her chin against her chest. "I've been so alone since you left. At least when Ma walked out, I still had you."

"Oh, I wish I could hug you."

"Me too." The sob that wracked her shoulders made me want to hurt our father for putting her through this. If he'd kept his mouth closed that day in the bar, Darian's people wouldn't have known about Nia's magic. None of this would have happened.

The idea of telling Darian about Nia's magic crossed my mind for a second. She'd live in the estate where she'd have a proper place to sleep and decent food. Plus Rahanna, Cam, and I could keep an eye on her. At least then we'd be together.

Reality shredded through the fairy tale I'd created in my brief fantasy. I would never, never let Nia be at Darian's mercy.

It felt like there was a fishhook in my sternum, tugging at me.

"I think I only have a few moments left." I wished I could cuddle her like I used to when we were both hurting. I wanted to heal her, make her know this wasn't her fault in any way. I could only think of one way. "Can you show me your magic? I know I said never to use it again, but please show me, just this one time."

Nia let out a ragged breath as she tried to keep the sobs locked up. Waving her hand, the doll twirled in the air, doing funny little moves. Watching her use magic to make the doll dance made me realize magic could be beautiful and good. It was upsetting that such a wonderful thing could cause so much trouble. But it wasn't the fault of the magic, or Nia. It was Darian and his greed that twisted it into something terrible.

After a few moments, the doll stuck its tattered arms out and performed a dramatic bow. Nia scooped it out of the air and clutched it to her chest. Her pain echoed into me as I again felt the tug of being called back to my body. I wasn't ready to leave her.

"That was beautiful. Your magic is beautiful." I rushed out the words, desperate for every last second. "I love you, kid."

"Love you too, big sis." Nia's arms tightened around the doll.

I flashed a sad smile before I felt my spirit disappear from the room. My vision blurred then pain crashed into me for a moment. It faded as my essence settled into my body again. My lungs burned as I gasped for air. Icy tingles spread through my fingers and toes as I shot up in the bed.

Ghost rubbed his hand over my leg, almost as though he were trying to soothe me through the jarring transition. His touch was a warm breath gusting over me.

I turned to him frantically. "Please help me escape. Your magic is so strong; there must be a way. I'll do anything."

"What happened? Is your sister okay?" he asked.

I swallowed hard. "For now. But I need to be there for her. I *need* her."

The light in his eyes grew flat and he drifted away from

me. "I can't."

I lunged off the bed toward him, stopping inches from his form. "Anything, I'll do anything. Please."

The ghost slumped as he looked at the ground. "I said I can't, Zari, not won't. I'm stuck here too. It's like there's something tethering me, keeping me in this building. I can't even get out into the grounds to try to do something to break the barrier spell out there."

The shame he felt was palpable. I wasn't sure why he wanted to help me so much, but deep down, I found myself wanting to ease his pain and confusion. He deserved to know what had happened to him. I took a long, calming breath and sat on the side of the bed.

"Thank you, for helping me see Nia. You want to try those names now?"

"Won't hurt to run them by me, I guess." He refused to meet my eyes as he fiddled with the corner of his hazy shirt.

I took my first shot. "Ethan?"

His eyes danced around as his mouth repeated the name, then he shook his head.

"What about Ronald? Or Allister?"

After a long pause, he shook his head.

"Are you sure?" Of course, it wouldn't be that easy, but I wished it was. His disappointment weighed on me.

"I'm sure. I have this feeling that if you said the right

name, I'd know it."

Despair settled in me. "I'll keep looking."

Ghost grew more transparent. "Only when it's safe. I don't want you to risk yourself."

When he was gone, I lay back on the bed, exhausted emotionally and physically. Then I heard one final whisper from my ghostly friend.

"If I could, I would free you in a heartbeat."

Sixteen

POUNDING ON MY door dragged me from a sleep I'd only just fallen into. Before I could get out of bed, it swung open, smashing against the wall. Darian stood in the doorway.

Fear skittered through me. He'd never come into the dorms before. Whenever he wanted to speak to anyone, he summoned them to his office. He seemed larger, more powerful, standing in my tiny room like this.

I blinked, blearily. It was early evening, and the sounds of other ritualists eating their dinner came from down the hall. I'd gone to bed early, still healing from the beating.

Darian flicked his hand at my roommate, and she scurried away. Whatever was happening was between me and Darian alone. I stood up from the bed, despite my every instinct making me want to hide under the covers like a child afraid of monsters in the dark. *There's no hiding from this monster.*

"I bet you're wondering why I'm here." Darian stepped closer, stealing more of my personal space. He wasn't smiling, and his whole face twitched. "Funny story. You see, my business partner, the son of the gold statue you gifted me? He came through for me in a spectacular way. Being the great guy I am, I thought I'd reward him, give him his father back."

Oh, no.

I knew where this was going, but had zero concept of what the consequences would be. Other than *bad*. Alarm bells went off in my brain as my heart raced, threatening to beat out of my chest.

"So, I touched the statue to revert the man back from gold, but nothing happened. Surprising, no?" Darian's icy gaze bore into me.

I tried to look shocked, but I wasn't, and I was sure Darian saw right through me. I always thought there'd be a risk someone would touch the statue, but hoped that since only Darian knew its origin, it wouldn't blow back on me. And I'd hoped he wouldn't touch it himself, too proud to lose the golden proof of his power.

I knew the statue wouldn't revert back into the man. Because it never *was* the man. It was only ever a magical construct created by Ghost and had nothing to revert back into.

A CAGE OF GOLD AND LIES

"Then I got to thinking about the whole thing. Turning a person into gold is far different than a bobbin of thread. Or even a dress. Even my best ritualist wouldn't be able to do that with years of practice and the right spells. I asked myself how this could be, and I can only come up with one answer."

He paused again, gazing down at me. He seemed to relish making my anxiety spiral out of control while waiting for his big reveal. "You're a thaumaturgist."

Cam's explanation of that spellborn type came back to me—once-in-a-generation rare, so rare he didn't even bother to elaborate.

Having Ghost create the statue had seemed like a good idea at the time. It had fit with my earlier lies, and was less sickening than trying to create some other proof of a murder. It had let me pretend I'd carried out the kill order, but now I realized I'd gone too far. It had looked too powerful.

I shook my head, trying to deny everything. "I don't even know what that is."

The warning in Darian's eyes was vivid. "You know, because it's what you've been doing this whole time! Thaumaturgists are the most powerful of the spellborn— miracle workers, who can shape magic without spells. They can turn a thought into reality." His eyes flashed, a greed and fury beyond any I'd seen before lighting them from within. My legs felt numb, wanting to crumble beneath me.

"I haven't seen one since …" Darian's words trailed off.

"Since what? What did you do to the last one?" My voice was all gasps.

Darian sneered silently and it felt like a dagger in my heart. "I'm not. I'm not a thaumaturgist!"

As the pitch of my voice had grown high, his grew low and hard. "You are. And you're going to be so, *very*, useful to me."

I searched for a way to escape, but Darian stood between me and the only door. I had no idea what I was going to do. I could only think about my very next move, and everything in me screamed to flee.

Dashing forward, I jumped around Darian, racing through the doorway and into the hall. Both ends if it were blocked by a couple of huge security goons. I charged one pair, hoping to slip through. Their hands wrapped around my arms, yanking me off my feet.

Screaming and thrashing, I was no match for the two muscled henchmen. There was worry in their eyes, as though I could use my supposed all-powerful magic on them at any moment. A bitter laugh echoed up through my completely unenchanted body. They pulled me toward the door leading out of the dorm.

I didn't know what Darian had planned for me, but it couldn't be good. As I was dragged out, Rahanna shuffled back, trying to put as much space between us as she could.

Cam stood next to her, a dark expression on his face. No one came to help me.

I kicked my feet out so they hooked onto either side of the doorframe, trying to hold on and prevent the henchmen from taking me across the threshold. They kicked back, heavy boots scraping and bruising my legs through the thin fabric of my uniform, stomping until I couldn't hold on any longer.

Why weren't they using magic to transport me out of there? Why the long, painful dragging fight? I glanced around, taking in all the terrified expressions of the spellborn in the common room. The answer clicked. Darian was making an example out of me by publicly removing me. The spellborn who were here would repeat it to the ones who weren't until all of them knew. The fact Darian had come in person made the statement even bolder.

My feet dragged across the ground as I got one last look at my friends and the other spellborn. Once we were through the door, I picked up my feet, hoping my deadweight would be enough to throw them off-balance so I could make a break for it.

For a moment, it worked. The stone path bit into my knees at the sudden contact as they almost dropped me. Then one of them grabbed both of my arms as the other clutched my feet. Even in this position I flailed for a few minutes, but it did nothing except exhaust me. They were too strong. Darian

followed along, a few steps behind, glaring at me.

They carried me like that all the way to the testing room where they tossed me into one of the glass cubes. Pain exploded in my side as I crashed into the legs of the table.

Darian stepped into my cell and stared down at me. "You're going to show me just how powerful you really are. No more lies. No more tricks. You have until morning. I expect you to create something so wonderful, I can't even tell you what it would be. You're smart. I know you won't dare disappoint me. You've disappointed me too much already."

He studied me for a long moment. I had nothing I could say, no idea how I could talk myself out of this. Darian seemed thoughtful in his anger, and when he slammed the door to lock me in, he went straight across to the high-security vault room instead of leaving.

I watched in defeat as he pressed the keypad, typing his entry code. The tune of the high-pitched beeps created a pattern in my brain. It sounded like the lullaby of death.

SEVENTEEN

FOR THE THIRD time in my life, Darian had me locked in a glass cell.

But this was the first time I wasn't scared of passing his test. I was sure Ghost would help me if he could. What did frighten me was what was going to happen to me afterwards, when Darian thought I was a thaumaturgist under his control. Ghost couldn't cover for me all the time.

And he wasn't showing. Minutes ticked on as I stood alone. Even with his help, what was I supposed to create to pass this test? Something so wonderful even Darian couldn't tell me what it was? I quadruple checked the chamber, but there wasn't a single spell or clue as to what I should make. Which made sense if he thought I was a thaumaturgist. They didn't need a spell to work magic.

I wasn't sure what the limitations of Ghost's magic were, whether he could fulfil the requirements. But I had a feeling he could.

Thinking back to when Ghost had turned the bobbin into golden thread, I'd noticed he didn't use words to do that. But maybe any conjurer could have done that. It could have been a simple illusion which broke when Darian touched it, but that wasn't the case for the statue. He'd created the golden statue of the man from magic alone.

Ghost hadn't uttered a word, and there was no way a conjurer could do that.

And shifting my very spirit out of my body just so I could visit with my sister? That sort of magic was breathtaking.

The thought of all he'd done for me made butterflies erupt in my belly. I wasn't sure how, but the ghost cared about what happened to me, and if I stopped lying to myself, I cared about him too. How could I not for someone who constantly tried to help me? Who showed me kindness and asked nothing in return? After so many years feeling alone, the idea of Ghost being with me gave me comfort I'd never found before.

I had to find out who he was. I had no new clues to his name, but now I knew something about him for sure. Ghost was a thaumaturgist. And it sounded like Darian knew who he was, may have even had a hand in his death. All I had to do now was find out the rest.

I put my palms against the glass, peering out. It had been maybe ten minutes since I was locked in here, but Ghost still hadn't arrived. Darian hadn't left the high-security area yet either. I wished I knew what was in there. I turned my back to the pane and slid down to the floor, hugging my knees and chewing my lips.

My pulse picked up as I pondered what could happen if I uncovered Ghost's identity.

As soon as I had his name, I'd tell him. Then … what? He was the first ghost I'd ever known, and the first anyone else I'd talked to had heard of. Anything could happen. Maybe he would still be around, but free, no longer stuck haunting this building. But I couldn't shake the worry that revealing his identity would mean he'd move on to whatever was after this life. An ache formed in my chest at the thought.

The vault door swung open and Darian stormed out, stomped by my cell without even glancing at me, and left down the hall.

A moment after he was gone, I heard Ghost's voice.

"Here we go again?" His tone was playful. He floated closer to where I sat, then moved back again, his hazy form sliding down the opposite wall to me. His spectral legs stretched out, almost reaching me in the small space.

"Yup. It seems to be a talent of mine. It's amazing I keep leading people to think I'm so powerful when I don't have a drop of magic myself."

"Oh, I don't know. I find you fairly enchanting," Ghost said softly.

My heart rate kicked up a notch, flushing warmth into my cheeks. No man had ever said something like that to me before.

No man had ever made me *feel* like this before.

I stared at his ghostly form. It was so easy to be with him. He was amazing, and I truly enjoyed his company, beyond what he could do for me or what I might owe to him.

But he was a ghost. Nothing could come from this. "Pretty sure the power is all yours. I haven't even found any new names for you to try."

He folded his legs and floated closer, genie-like, until he rested against the wall beside me. "You know, I only made the request because you kept asking. In a way, I was actually indulging you, again." His voice was deep, teasing, and playful.

"Gee, thanks, just add that to my bill then." I rolled my eyes.

He chuckled. "You know I'd help you without any repayment."

"I do." He was such a sweet soul. He deserved his own happiness, and I wanted to be the person to help him. "But

I still want to give you something in return.”

"You give me your company.”

"I want to give you more.” The words came out breathless.

Ghost stilled in place, watching me for a long moment. "So do I,” he whispered.

My pulse felt like a bird, trying to flap free from my throat.

Ghost faded as he turned away from me again, shrugging and clearing his throat. "If you want to guess a few names, go ahead. You never know. We might get lucky.”

I blinked slowly, took a deep breath. "Okay, sure. Names.” I racked my brain trying to think of some, but suddenly it was blank. They didn't have to mean anything; I just needed a name. I said the first one that came to mind. "Edmond?”

The ghost's eyes widened. "I hope not! How old do I look?” He pulled at what appeared to be his modern button-up shirt and slacks. His gaze returned to me with a playfully outrageous look. "I can't be Edmond old.”

"Gerald?” His mouth dropped open at the suggestion, so I continued. "Ernest, Wilbur, Jeremiah, Reginald?”

"Oh man, I hope it's none of those. Are you having a go at me?”

A strange feeling curled around my lips, lifting them. Was I actually being cheeky? Enjoying myself? Was I actually … flirting? I narrowed my eyes with concentration. "Vladimir, Ignatius, Mordecai?”

Ghost shook his head, his grin also growing.

I declared another guess in a booming, regal tone. "Rumpelstiltskin?"

"Wow." Ghost gasped.

My body went rigid with concern. "That wasn't it, was it?"

"No. I mean your smile. It's incredible." He paused, floating closer. "You're incredible."

Heat flushed my cheeks. My fingers moved to my lips as though I needed to feel the proof of the curve of them myself. *He thinks I'm incredible.* I didn't know what to think, what to do.

Ghost chuckled, clearly pleased he'd knocked me speechless. "This has been fun, getting to see some of the real Zari. And I appreciate you trying to help me, but really, it's not a big deal. If you discover my name, then, great. If not, I'll still do anything I can to help you."

I whispered, "Why?"

There were so many questions in that one word. Why would he do so much for a stranger with nothing in return? Why did he keep coming to me right when I needed him? Why me? I was nobody to him, and not nearly worth the trouble I'd become. *Why did he think I was incredible?*

Ghost rested his hand on my knee, light as a feather. "Because you're worth it. I don't have to know you to see you deserve a little help."

I wiped at my cheek, hoping he hadn't seen the tears that

had fallen, then I let out a breathy laugh. "Okay, so tonight I have a new impossible challenge. Want to hear it?"

"Is anything truly impossible when we put our minds together?" He leaned against the cell wall, but didn't remove his hand from my leg. The barely-there warmth of his touch sent hot swirls through my stomach. His closeness gave me strength.

"I have to make something so wonderful even words can't describe it."

The ghost's facial expression didn't change as he watched me intently. "That's all? Well, why didn't you tell me that the moment I appeared." He cracked his knuckles, then put two fingers from his free hand against his temple and wrinkled his nose in concentration. I wanted to look around the cell, to see what he was creating, but his eyes held mine. "Hmm, it's not working. Oh, no wonder I can't create something so wonderful; you're already here."

"You're such a dork!" A giggle chased my words. I slapped a hand over my mouth to stifle the unexpected sound, but a snort broke out of me.

Ghost and I locked eyes.

"Don't you dare ... make a big deal ... out of that." My words shook with the tremors of suppressed laughter.

Ghost's eyes sparkled in gleeful defiance. "Hush! Did you hear that? The elusive Zari laugh. They're so rare, thus far only rumors told of possible findings. Could I be the first valiant adventurer to have experienced the real thing?"

I swatted at him and my hand went straight through, pinging on the glass.

"Ha!" Ghost barked.

I snorted again and doubled over as I tried to contain myself. Every stress, every frustration, seemed to burst out of me in a mass of relieving laughter. I lost it all over again when I heard the contagious giggles spread to Ghost. I finally composed myself, wiping tears of laughter off my aching cheeks.

Ghost watched me, grinning, with a light shining behind his eyes. "Sounded like you needed that."

"Yeah, I guess I did. It felt good. It felt free." I rearranged myself back into a cross-legged position, and was disappointed that Ghost's hand was no longer on my knee.

Once I'd stilled again, he moved a little closer, his shoulder up against mine. A wave of butterflies fluttered through my belly. "What would you do if you were free?"

"I'd find Nia and get us both far away from Oramont." But then I wouldn't see Ghost again. People like him were rare, and the idea of spending the rest of my life without him made me sad. I loved my sister, but I had to be a different person for her. I had been the responsible one, the protector, for so long I'd forgotten myself, forgotten how to laugh.

Ghost had given that back to me.

"Of course, but if you could go anywhere after this, where would it be?"

"If I didn't have a care in the world and the money to spend?" I paused for dramatic effect, enjoying the way he seemed to hang on my every word. I wasn't used to being the center of attention. "I'd go to Venice. I've seen pictures of it in books and always wanted to visit. Or live there if I could."

"Really? What would you do there?" He stuck his free arm behind his head, his gaze never leaving my face.

I yawned, and shuffled farther down the glass as I imagined the answer to Ghost's question. "It would be so wonderful to see all the beautiful buildings, all that history and culture in one small place." I winced a little and shrugged as I made the decision to open up. "It's going to sound dumb, but I really wanted to be a singing gondolier. When I was a kid, I ripped a picture out of an old magazine. I'm not sure why I did it at the time, but it was just so beautiful, and I needed to dream of something good in my life. It was a photo of a gondolier, pushing through beneath a bridge, singing to a couple in the boat. For years I kept that picture hidden away, sneaking glances at it, imagining myself there. I would even sing to myself, practicing just in case. It was a stupid dream, but that's what dreams are for—letting yourself hope for the silliest thing that could never happen."

Ghost frowned. "I thought dreams were good to believe in, as something to work toward."

Maybe for some people. Those with resources, a supportive family, who weren't just struggling not to starve. "Dreams don't come true. Not for people like me."

Ghost moved back, turning to face me directly. The intensity of his gaze felt like a clamp around my chest.

His voice was a hushed whisper. "Don't say that. You don't know what the future has in store for you."

Eighteen

PANIC BURST THROUGH me as I bolted awake.

I'd fallen asleep talking to Ghost! And it was the real thing, not that half-dozing nap I normally had. There might even have been a bit of drool on my shirt.

I frantically thought back, and anxiety crashed into me when I realized we never finished discussing the test and how we were going to complete it.

The sound of Darian clearing his throat sent razor shards through my veins. My eyes found the source of the noise and I cringed away from my captor, waiting for his wrath.

Except the expression on his face looked smug, not furious. His eyes glanced behind me, so I followed them.

Standing before the back cell wall was a huge slab of gold.

The front was decorated in an intricate low-relief style—a scene with narrow, two-story buildings separated by canals. Tiny people were visible in the ornate arched windows and balconies, and on the bridges that spanned the water.

At the very front of the design, a larger gondola floated near a statue of a winged lion.

The most jaw-dropping part was that the entire creation was alive. Each of the people looped through a series of motions. A woman hung her laundry on ropes outside her window. Tourists checked their maps and took photos. Smaller gondolas in the background bobbed and slid over the golden water. It was so detailed I could see little fish swimming.

In the gondola in the foreground, the gondolier was missing the stereotypical striped shirt. The woman pushing the boat instead wore a beautiful dress with long, soft ruffles. She appeared to be singing. Her passenger was a man, sitting next to her, watching with a look of rapture on his face.

My throat closed up from the sight of it.

It's me.

Or at least who I could have been in some other life. Not only had Ghost listened to what I'd said and encouraged my foolish dreams, he'd used them to create this display of indescribable magic.

Darian looked at the artwork as though it was my delivery to him, but I understood deep down inside me that this was

A CAGE OF GOLD AND LIES

Ghost's gift to me. *Ghost did all of this for me.*

"I knew you wouldn't disappoint me." Darian held his arms wide while he spoke. "This is proof you can perform true magic to create miracles. This is great news! I've been looking for a new thaumaturgist since I had to destroy the last one for being uncooperative. You won't make me do that to you, will you? Not now that you understand I control everything in your life you hold dear."

Ghost. It was true then; Darian was to blame for Ghost's death. I gulped my emotions down and spoke flatly. "I understand."

Darian grinned widely, white teeth flashing as bright as the golden scene. He stepped closer to me, then placed a small, black velvet box on the table. "You've earned a present."

I stared at it like it was venomous. I'd seen boxes like this in a jewelry store window, but I didn't think for a moment he'd gotten me something like that. Hair stood up on the back of my neck. Darian didn't give gifts. The last time he'd given me something, it was a day off from work so I could think about what I'd done wrong while feeling the full humiliation of my pain. Whatever was inside that velvet box wouldn't be good. It would be a reminder of his power, because that was the only thing that Darian cared about.

I didn't want to open that box.

"Go ahead. Open it." His words were playful, coaxing,

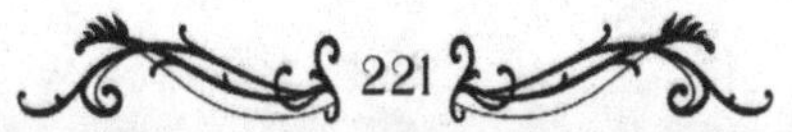

but they were clearly a demand.

I suppressed the shiver that ran through me and picked up the soft case. I braced myself, but nothing could have prepared me for what was inside.

As the lid hinged open with a soft snap, my world tilted. The sting of acid in my throat brought tears to my eyes.

On the black velvet inside the box laid a severed finger.

Instead of the normal pink undertones of flesh, it was a pale-yellow color. I clutched the table for support when I saw the wedding ring with a tiny dent in the side closest to where the hand should be.

That's Pa's wedding ring.

Bile threatened to burst out of me, but I swallowed it back.

"Just a little reminder for you so you don't forget." Darian smiled benevolently, as though he'd given me diamond earrings.

I had been so worried about Nia this whole time, and as much as Sergio and I had our issues, he was still my pa, still family. I still loved him. Seeing proof that Darian had hurt him pained me in just the way he'd planned. Dread froze me as another thought crashed into my mind. What if next time Darian delivered a box with a piece of Nia inside it? She was too young and innocent for Darian's level of psychopathy.

I looked at him, unable to hide my emotions. Did he see fear, anger, or hate?

"Don't worry. Your family is okay. For now. As long as you remember your place and do as you're told. I won't suffer unruly servants." He reached out to my hands and snapped the lid of the box closed again, then watched me expectantly. When I didn't budge, he pointed to the left pocket of my pants. Swallowing back my anger and disgust, I clenched my jaw while I tucked it away.

Darian was a disgusting savage. His reign of terror had to end.

"Now that we're on the same page, I have a job that requires a truly gifted thaumaturgist such as yourself." Darian spoke in a soft tone, as though we were sharing secrets. "I want you to get rid of Peldin for me. He's embarrassed me and my family name long enough and the only way to correct the harm he's done is to remove him. I don't mean kill him—I want him *erased*. You and I should be the only people to know he ever existed."

I gasped. How could he ask that, how could he want that for his own family? Did he have no love or compassion in him at all? "Your brother?"

Darian's eyes flashed dangerously at the word.

I shouldn't have been surprised. Nothing was too evil for Darian. He would kill someone over a business deal. Why wouldn't he want to get rid of his own brother to end the gossip against his family name?

Another question also terrified me. Would even a thaumaturgist be powerful enough to erase someone's existence?

Darian watched me, expecting my answer.

I stumbled over my words while I tried to find some way out of this. "How would I do that? I'm not sure I'm powerful enough. Creating this golden scene took everything I had. To erase a life from existence … I'm not sure anyone could do that."

Darian rolled his eyes at me. "You'll work it out. You've proven to be surprisingly resourceful." He closed the distance between us, patting the box in my pocket that contained my father's finger. His hot breath wafted over my face as he spoke. "You've also proven to enjoy making excuses and telling lies. So, I'm giving you twenty-four hours to find that resourcefulness of yours and get this done."

Darian stepped clear of my way and pointed out of the cell. "Now, you know where to find him."

I walked away, clutching my shaking fingers together. A sick feeling flooded through me until I felt like I might drown.

My emotions warred as I tried to think of a way out of this horrible situation. I couldn't do what Darian asked, and I refused to ask it of Ghost.

But if I didn't, I'd be forfeiting my family's lives.

Nineteen

"WHAT ARE YOU doing here?" There was a tone of pleasant surprise in Peldin's rough voice. It only piled onto the weight already threatening to break me.

He was alone in his room, and I wasn't sure if he or Darian had sent away the carer who was meant to be there. The state of the place suggested no one had cared for Peldin in a while.

The first thing I did was snatch the gift box from my pocket and throw it in the rubbish. I couldn't have it near me a moment longer. *Pa's finger.* It felt wrong throwing it away, like a symbol that all our lives were garbage to Darian, but what else could I do?

Peldin watched me curiously but didn't question me again.

I dragged myself over to the chair next to his and collapsed into it. *What do I do now?* How did I tell Peldin that his own brother had sent me to get rid of him? I couldn't *not* tell him though. He deserved at least to know, and a lot more.

I churned through my plans and options. Maybe with Ghost's help we could steal Peldin out of the estate, make everyone forget he existed, and keep him hidden somewhere. But in order for that to work, he'd have to remain hidden and completely alone for the rest of his years. It would be even worse than his life now. And I didn't know how to get him out of this estate in the first place. It was beyond even Ghost's powers. I scrubbed at my scalp until my hair came loose from its bun. I couldn't see how to make this work.

With a frustrated grunt, I leaned forward in my chair, elbows resting on my knees. "Your … Darian gave me a new job."

"And?" Peldin's hard eyes were a tiny bit softer today, but he still looked like a grumpy recluse.

"I'm supposed to remove you entirely from existence." My words flew out in a rush, completely unfiltered. I cringed at the harshness of them, waiting for him to lash out at me in anger. When he didn't immediately start yelling, I relaxed a bit.

Peldin set the book he'd been reading open-side down on the table. "You look like you thought I wasn't expecting this. Although I figured Darian would be smarter about it. If I was erased as though I never was, how would he know

the job was done?"

"Only he and I are supposed to know about it."

Peldin turned away, his head wobbling on a weak neck as he nodded slowly. He shrugged, but only the shoulder he wasn't slumped onto moved. "As long as you remember me, it won't be so bad."

"I'm not going to do it!" I snapped.

"Ah, come on. No one's going to miss me." His wrinkled lips pulled up on one side, but there was a deep sadness there that I couldn't ignore. It was as though he'd already given up, a long time ago.

"Don't talk like that. *I* would miss you."

Peldin glared sharply at me, then down at his crumpled body. "You'd really miss this?"

"I'd miss the man who, despite his own problems in this house of horrors, was kind to me." I wanted to cheer him up, to chase away some of that defeatist attitude, but I really did mean what I said. "Anyway, even if I wanted to get rid of you, which I don't, I wouldn't be able to."

He tilted his head to one side as he looked me over. "Everyone's been talking, saying you're one of the most powerful spellborn alive—maybe even a thaumaturgist. You could sneeze wrong and I'd disappear."

"What? Really?" Was Ghost actually that powerful? It made me wonder what Peldin knew. "Did you know the last

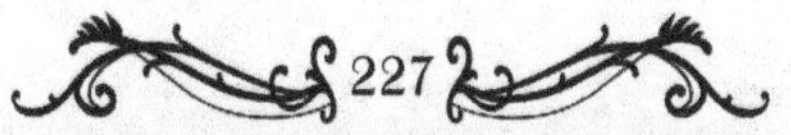

thaumaturgist? The one here at the estate, until Darian … killed him?"

Peldin's eyes glazed over as he considered my question. He shook his head, frowning deeply. "There was a thaumaturgist here? I don't remember. But it sounds like something my brother would do. And all the more reason you need to do everything he says, now that he knows you're one."

I shook my head while shame washed through me. What would he think if he knew I'd lied this whole time? Was it safe to tell him?

"Stop torturing yourself over this and just do it. You need to focus on getting far away from here. Go find your family and get them to safety, no matter what you have to do to me." His winter-blue gaze held mine steadily, not a hint of indecision in his tone. "Give up on me. I have."

"When I say I can't, I mean I really *can't*." I rubbed my face with my hands in frustration. "I'm not spellborn at all. From the moment I arrived, I haven't been able to cast a single spell."

"How——"

"Someone's been helping me."

Peldin put a hand up. "I understand. You don't want to reveal and endanger them. Even when it's your life on the line." Peldin eyed me, a frown appearing over his soft eyes, exaggerating the wrinkles. He cleared his throat. "I want you to run. Escape this place before Darian finds out."

I laughed at him. "There's no way out! I only have twenty-four hours. I can't plan an escape in that time."

Peldin gripped the arm of the chair I sat in. He leaned toward me, using his finger to urge me to move closer to him. When I was only a few inches away, his lips opened. "You don't need a plan because I made one for you."

"Are you serious?"

He nodded and slumped back into the chair again, as though he'd expended all his energy. "After what happened, the other night …" His eyes cast over the still aching bruises on my face. "… I started searching for a way out, and I found something."

"A weakness in the barrier?" I asked warily, remembering how Rahanna's escape had been nothing more than a lesson. I leaned away from Peldin. "Are you testing me?"

He shook his head so vehemently his whole body moved with it. "No, it's not one of Darian's traps; I've checked myself. It's a flaw in the spell. Through an old treehouse that's somehow breaking a gap in the wall. I don't think anyone has been in there since Darian and I were kids."

My mouth went dry. I stared at Peldin, speechless. Did I really dare to have hope?

He looked from me down to the ground. "It was a happier time back then … so it's only fitting now that it could bring

me the last bit of happiness I'll ever know."

Peldin could have escaped without telling me about the way out, but he'd stayed to help me. Just like the ghost, Peldin had gone out of his way for me when I had nothing to give him in return.

But unlike Ghost, Peldin's body was free to leave this place too. I scooped his bony hands into mine. "Come with me."

Peldin's fingers shook, and he looked at me with a heartbreaking smile. "I can't do that. I'd only slow you down. Even if we got away, I don't want to burden you with my broken body."

I shook my head, forgetting for a moment that he was mostly bound to his wheelchair. But I didn't care. I'd grown to care for him, and I didn't want to leave him behind. He was a good man and shouldn't have to suffer, always wondering when Darian would succeed at getting rid of him for good.

"We'll work something out. I … I can help carry you when you need it."

"It's okay, Zari." He squeezed my hands in return, weakly. "You're going to leave me behind, and it's okay. Don't worry about me. All I want is your safety. Until I met you, I'd forgotten how to want anything." A hint of pink colored his normally pale cheeks.

My heart broke. It was clear he wasn't going to come with me, and I couldn't force him. I leaned over and hugged him

briefly. When we broke apart, we both cleared our throats awkwardly, looking away.

The rest of our time with each other was awkward but special.

We spent the day together, deciding it was best to wait until nightfall to cover my escape. The time was mostly quiet, reading in each other's company, or chatting softly about mundane things: likes and dislikes, the weather, a song that had once made us feel like so much more than mere mortals. Sometimes frustration would drive me to pacing and I would rant, trying to convince Peldin to come with me, but he wouldn't budge. I wondered aloud if I could go to Rahanna or Cam and bring them along instead, but Peldin warned me against it. It was already a huge risk. I had to go alone. Peldin would do his best to cover for me, and I was sure Ghost would too, but if more spellborn were missing the alarm would raise so much sooner.

When it became dark outside and fewer people moved around, it was time. Excitement filled me, but also another strange and deep feeling that this was all somehow wrong.

"I'll never forget you," I told Peldin.

I knelt before him, squeezing his hands in mine. I didn't want to let go, but with a soft grumble of goodbye, he pulled away from me, staring only at the ground.

Giving him one last look, I left his humble room.

Walking like I was supposed to be there, I strode down the stairways and through the estate. I passed a few conjurers working late cleaning shifts, but nobody questioned me or stopped me with my ritualist uniform on and hood up. I hoped Ghost would appear, that I could say goodbye to him, but I was rarely out of sight of any other person.

It was only when I reached the bottom end of the estate's gardens, where the trees were taller and fewer garden lights spotlighted the topiary, that I was completely alone. Then I picked up my pace, unable to continue the rouse of nonchalance. I might actually be getting out of here. I couldn't wait a second longer.

The treehouse was exactly where Peldin had said it would be. A once grand wooden fort, it had grown weak and slumped to the side, much like Peldin's body. The timber was weathered and gray, and it was obvious that once, a long time ago, the brothers had spent many hours playing there. They'd worn down the middle of the wooden slats used for the ladder, drawn on the walls, pinned up flags and mementos.

I tested the slats with my weight, and climbed as speedily as I dared. One gave way and I almost fell. When I made it into the fort, I had to crawl to fit through it.

Inside on one of the walls, two sets of initials had been carved. *P.K.* and *D.K.* Right under their initials were tiny handprints in black paint. It was so sweet and innocent. They must have had some love for each other back then.

I placed my hand over Peldin's print. What had gone so wrong between the brothers?

Pushing myself forward, I moved toward the back wall of the fort where some of the boarding had fallen free, making a hole that looked down over a grassy field to a roadway. I shuffled toward where the barrier should be and reached out my hand. My hair didn't stand up like it had before. Leaning forward, I passed through the perimeter line. There was nothing there. The barrier simply didn't exist here. I could move right through with no effect at all.

Three steps—that was the distance between me and the world outside the estate.

But I couldn't move.

I imagined Peldin making this climb, how hard he must have worked and searched to find this gap. He'd risked everything to find this for me to escape through, so why couldn't I force my feet to take me to freedom … to my sister?

I wanted freedom. More than anything, it was what I always wanted. But would I really gain that by running back to my old life?

The truth left a bitter taste in my mouth. I hadn't been free before I was stolen to this place. My last cage was poverty. I didn't have the freedom to go to school, get a decent job, or live in a real home. I hadn't been free even before Ma left

us. There was no more freedom outside these walls than there was inside them. I'd lived in a prison of responsibility, of survival, only looking out for myself and Nia, and never even free to make a deeper connection with anyone else.

Now Darian thought I was a thaumaturgist. He'd never stop hunting me. And I felt something else now too. I no longer wanted to be the kind of person who only looked out for herself and her family. Ghost had helped me, no matter what. I had him, Peldin, Rahanna, and Cam to thank for so much, and I had grown to care for them all. I didn't want them to suffer here. I didn't want that for the kind conjurer who had shown me the ropes, or the sisters with their secret, or my snoring roommate. Not *anyone*.

Until something changed, Darian was going to keep hurting people. Maybe I could be the kind of person who could risk it all to save them, and save every life that Darian would take in the future. No matter what happened to me, and—I gulped a sob—even what happened to my family, Darian had to be stopped, or he would continue breaking others, breaking families and hearts, for whatever the duration of his life could be.

I thought of Lainey, and how I'd sworn to myself I would remember her, draw strength from her, when it came to my escape. Instead, I found a new clarity inside me.

I wasn't going to run.

A CAGE OF GOLD AND LIES

I was going to do everything in my power to end Darian King's reign.

Peldin had given me more than just this chance to escape; he'd given me hope. Because if this gap in the barrier was here, then there might also be a flaw in Darian's protection spell.

A plan formed in my mind of a possible way to defeat Darian. It was risky, and it would only work if I stayed here. I'd only get one shot, and it either worked or I wouldn't have another chance to use this escape route. I looked again out the hole that led to freedom, then backed away. After all I'd been through here, I wasn't satisfied with solely trying to survive anymore; I needed to *really* live. And I would fight for that. Otherwise, what was the point?

I hoped I could trust the friends I'd made here, because I was going to need their help. This was my first plan I could do without Ghost, but I hoped to see him again anyway. I thought about all he'd done to protect me, and the hours we'd spent talking. He'd always tried cheering me up with his silly jokes, and then he'd gifted me that most incredible scene from my dreams. It made me feel so much toward him. And made me want to fulfill my promise to him.

If I was going to do that, I had to try now, because my plan to stop Darian was likely to get me killed.

I climbed down from the treehouse, dashing back through the shadowy gardens. I'd have to hurry because I didn't have

much time before Darian would come to see the results of the task he'd set me—to erase Peldin. Less than twenty-four hours to save Ghost, then save *everybody*. No problem, right?

My first goal was to find out what secrets were hidden behind that high-security door. There must be something powerful in that vault, and what was more powerful than a thaumaturgist?

Maybe Darian was hiding something back there related to Ghost.

TWENTY

IT MUST HAVE been well past midnight as I snuck back through the corridors of the estate. The atrium I had gone through on my first day had an all new artwork hanging where the tapestry I saw created had been hung. It was a portrait of Darian, again, standing atop a golden pyramid like an Egyptian god. Another display of his extravagance—having the ritualists create incredible works of art only to destroy and replace them.

Even fewer people were about now, so I moved slowly and casually, hoping to anyone watching that I appeared to simply be another ritualist on her way to a late shift. I made it to the gilt elevator and descended down to the testing area. It wasn't hard to find my way there alone. I'd been there enough times.

Now, in the large warehouse-like space, I hurried, dashing by the glass cube cells to the vault-like door. I was grateful, though surprised, that the keypad wasn't more futuristic with a fingerprint or iris scanner. Maybe Darian was too confident in his power to worry. Knowing he wasn't spellborn either was a comfort too; the only security should be mundane if he could unlock it on his own.

I closed my eyes for a moment, humming through the tune the buttons had made when I'd seen Darian type in his code. Pressing all the numbers in a row, I got a feel for which number had which tone. I crossed my fingers that I wasn't going to get locked out of the system from wrong tries or set off some kind of alarm. Singing the pattern aloud, I pressed the corresponding buttons. When I finished the code, I held my breath and waited.

A soft buzz emanated from the box as the light turned green. Then the lock on the door clicked.

I let out a slow breath of relief and slipped through. Easing the door closed behind me, I made sure it latched again to cover my tracks. In all my time spent in the glass testing cells, I'd never seen anyone but the old conjurer and Darian come and go from this high-security area, and was happy when my guess that there weren't guards inside was confirmed.

I just hoped now there'd actually be something valuable in there.

A CAGE OF GOLD AND LIES

I also hoped what I'd find weren't the gruesome remains of a thaumaturgist, their body kept locked away, forcing them to haunt this place. It's what I half expected. If it was, at least it might bring answers.

The air was stale and had a tangy, unwashed smell. Inside the concrete-lined vault room there was another glass cell, decked out like a prison with a ratty, narrow bed, toilet and sink. Could this have been where Darian kept Ghost? Where he destroyed him?

The cell appeared to be empty. Then something moved. A ragged figure was huddled in a corner. A sour taste invaded my mouth.

"Hello?" I called softly.

They turned, no doubt curious about an unfamiliar voice. It was a woman, with long black hair and round, worried eyes.

My heart slammed so hard inside me I stumbled back into the wall.

I covered my hand with my mouth, trying to process what I saw, the face of a woman who had once been my whole world, my shining sun, my protector and heart. The woman who I thought had abandoned me.

"Ma?" The sound croaked from my distorted lips.

She looked at me for what felt like an eternity. "Zari? Is that you?"

I rushed to the cell wall and crouched down to get a

closer look. My hands pressed on the glass. "Ma!" It was all I could say, all I could do not to cry.

She scooted across the floor to where I was, pressing the glass from the other side.

"Baby! My baby!" she cried. "Why are you here? You shouldn't be here."

"What … How … Have you been in here this whole time?"

Her nod was small and crooked. "Look at you. You've grown so much. I'm so sorry."

"It's not your fault!" I didn't know exactly what had happened to her, but I knew that much for certain.

Her gaze grew sharp as daggers. "Zari, you have to go. You need to get out right now, or they will keep you too."

I had to swallow back my tears. "It's too late. I'm already one of Darian's prisoners."

Her hands curled into fists. "Nia? Sergio?"

"They're … okay." *For now.* I didn't want to go into details and distress Ma any further.

She sniffed as she shoved her stringy hair out of her face. "I'm so sorry. I didn't want to leave you. You must know now what he does. He learns of our magic, he takes us, and he keeps us. And he makes us do terrible things."

Pure fury raged through my veins. Darian had not only stolen my mother away, he'd ruined my love for her. When we'd accepted she wasn't coming back, a deeper part of me had begun to hate her for abandoning us, for everything I became responsible for in her absence.

But it had never been her fault.

Every other thought fled from me except one. To smash my mother out of this cell, out of this horrible prison, and hurry her to the gap in the barrier. We would get Nia—maybe even Sergio—and we'd make our escape. Even if it meant a life on the run. No matter what it meant. I wanted my mother back. I wanted my family whole.

"We have to get you out of there." I scrambled at the locked door, eyes darting for the mechanism that opened it.

"No. It's alarmed if you don't know the code!" Ma warned. I spotted the keypad. It was the same model as the main door, so I took the bet I had to have at least a couple of guesses before the alarm went off. I tried the same code as the other one, but the lights buzzed red.

I slammed my hands desperately against the glass. "Why has he got you locked up in here?"

"Because of what he made me do. I did something so terrible for him, an ancient spell of destruction. I didn't want to! But he threatened you. He threatened my baby girls."

Darian had known about Nia and I all along—he just didn't realize one of us had the ability to control magic until Pa messed up and blurted it out at the bar. No wonder they'd come for us so quickly. It also explained why he'd kept pushing me to cast more intricate magic and expressed disappointment when I failed. He'd known it ran in the family all along, because he'd had my mother here in a cell for six years.

I nodded solemnly. I knew exactly how powerful his threats were. I longed to wrap my arms around my mother. "Hang on, a spell of destruction? Was it to destroy a thaumaturgist?"

Ma frowned, her head tilted. "How did you know? It was designed to steal magic from a spellborn and destroy them. The moment Darian realized the spell worked, he threw me in here so I couldn't tell anyone."

My breath trembled. This was it. This is what had happened to Ghost. A destruction spell, cast by my own mother, at Darian's command.

Ma continued, "I think the only reason he's kept me alive is because he's worried that if I die, the magic I'd cast would unravel. Then the thaumaturgist would remember, would be free to retaliate against him."

Unravel? Surely the thaumaturgist couldn't come back from the dead. It didn't make sense. With my heart pounding in my throat, I asked, "Do you know who the man was? The target of the spell?"

Ma shrugged, clearly confused about my line of questioning. "No, I never met him."

All the rising hope disappeared.

"The spell only required his name."

And then, like a tidal wave, hope returned.

Ma looked thoughtful. "I still remember the spell, if that will help. I'm good at remembering rhymes like that."

"Me too," I whispered in a small sob. "And it will help." I nodded an encouragement to her.

Ma's face was too pale, too gaunt, as she licked her cracked lips and recited the words.

"Avaunt spirit, overbrimmed.

Recollection reduced, destroyed, dimmed.

Ruin Pel, steal his skin,

Cast forth all magic from within."

Time stopped around me.

Pel? *Peldin?* All the pieces of the puzzle fell together. Peldin's illness began around the same time my mother had disappeared. The same time Ghost started haunting these halls.

Peldin was the thaumaturgist Darian couldn't control.

I could only imagine Darian and all his greed, knowing he wasn't even spellborn, discovering his own brother was gifted a power so strong it only occurred once in a generation— and knowing he was set to inherit the King fortune too. So Darian had found a way to destroy him, to separate his magic from his body, take everything from him. He left his brother broken, trapped, unaware who he once was, all spirit gone.

But not dead.

Ghost isn't dead. My heart burst into overdrive. I'd been worried that when I discovered his identity, he would move on and disappear. *But he's not a ghost at all.* He was a powerful thaumaturgist, locked out of his physical form. Two halves of a whole. Two men I cared about who were one and the same. Both cursed, unable to remember why.

Maybe with his name, he could return to his body and become whole again.

"Zari? Are you okay?" Ma pawed at the glass, worried.

"I have to go. There's something I have to do. But I'll come back for you as soon as I can. I promise."

"Be careful. I love you." She kissed her fingers, then placed them against the glass of her cell. I pressed my hand against the glass again, vowing to succeed.

I would free her. I would free Ghost, Peldin, everyone.

And I would take Darian down at the same time for everything he had done.

TWENTY-ONE

"Ghost?" I called again, as I had every few moments after leaving the cell where my mother was kept. Why wasn't he appearing?

Worry made me reckless. He hadn't appeared to me all night, despite my crazy running around. Had he been watching, listening in while invisible as he had at other times? Then why not show himself to me now? I ran along the corridors, heading to Peldin's rooms, desperately calling for Ghost every few moments.

The echo of footsteps chased me. I swore, sprinting faster down the hallway, and darted to the left into another one. The elevator was the other way, the direction the pursuers came from, but I was heading to the servants' stairs anyway.

A giant of a man stepped out in front of me. I slid to a stop, then spun around.

More security guards lined up before me, blocking my path.

"Zari, Mr. King is going to be very disappointed in this behavior." Mr. Shaw's voice bounced down the hallway as he stepped to the front of the men. "You've broken his trust and the rules of the house. Now you must face your punishment."

I didn't wait for him to finish talking. I'd heard enough of these threats. I barreled toward them, hoping to charge through. I caught an elbow to my ribs as I smashed my body through a gap between two of the goons. Winded but still moving, I tumbled forward.

But then I heard familiar spell words spoken, and ropes appeared from nowhere. They tripped up my running legs, and I fell on my face. The bindings wound their way up my body, squeezing me so tight I struggled to breathe. *Ghost, where are you?*

Mr. Shaw loomed over me, smug as his boss.

I drew my wrapped body into a fetal position, then kicked out as hard as I could, cracking both feet into his knees. They bent backwards and he howled in pain, collapsing onto his back.

"Who's next?" I spat ferally from the ground.

With a grunt, Mr. Shaw waved his hand, repeating his spell. The ropes grew tighter, so tight they squeezed tears from my eyes and the last bit of breath out of my lungs. I gasped uselessly. My vision sparkled then grew dark.

Through blurry eyes, I saw the men cry and cower back.

The ropes disappeared from me. Oxygen screamed back into my chest.

I looked up to see Ghost. Pale, but there, standing protectively over me.

With a flick of his wrists, the men vanished. Only Mr. Shaw remained, dragged into the air like a marionette on invisible strings. His mouth was wide open in terror. Then he was gone too.

He'd revealed himself to save me. The enormity of the gesture left me dumbstruck for a moment. It didn't matter if people knew now, but Ghost didn't know that yet.

Ghost wavered in front of me, almost disappearing himself before returning. "I would have sent them to the other side of the world if I could. But for now they are locked away on the estate, and won't remember why. Are you okay?"

"Yeah, thank you." I stared at him in awe. He was more ghostly than I'd ever seen him, barely there. But now I knew who he was, I could almost see some of Peldin in him.

He reached out a hand as though to help me up, and then bashfully withdrew it. His eyes focused on me, looking over my body like he was reassuring himself he'd arrived in time. "I'm sorry I wasn't here sooner. I'm not sure where I was. Tonight has been … wrong somehow. I've been finding it harder to be around, to stay conscious, like I'm slipping away."

I propped myself up on my elbows and frowned. Was there something wrong with him?

When I remained on the ground, Ghost lowered himself down to my level. "I'm sorry I wasn't around to clean up the security feed. It's hard even now, keeping myself here."

His words faded in and out.

I was worried, but I wasn't sure why. What could possibly hurt Ghost?

Then I realized. Not Ghost … *Peldin. Oh, no.*

The things he'd said to me, when he'd told me to go without him, the way he'd seemed to have lost all hope. Horror unfurled inside me, its cold tendrils tracing to my every extremity. *Please no …* He wouldn't have given in entirely, would he? *I shouldn't have left him.*

Ghost turned clear as air in front of me and I lurched forward for him. "Ghost!"

What if Peldin was dying right now?

"Come back, please! I know who you are!" I cried.

The barest mist swirled in front of me. I couldn't make out any of his features. "You worked it out? I should have known. You're such a clever woman."

He spoke kindly, casually, not understanding the urgency. Unable to understand. Panic burned through my veins. I had to tell him now so he could save himself if he needed to. If he could.

"Your name is—"

His eyes grew wide and he vanished.

"Peldin! Your name is Peldin," I cried at the empty air.

I brushed long strands of hair out of my face as I caught my breath. Was I too late?

Please, please I can't be too late.

I scrambled to my feet and ran for the servants' stairs that led to Peldin's rooms. Maybe I was wrong, worrying for nothing. Maybe if I wasn't, there'd be something I could do. If I wasn't too late. Pain spiked through me as I pushed my body to the limit, taking three steps at a time until I reached Peldin's floor.

I turned the corner and almost tripped over my own feet.

A flash of light and crack of thunder sounded and before me stood a man. He wore the same tan slacks and white shirt I'd last seen Peldin in, but he stood tall and—mostly—straight. There was still a slight lean to one side, the side Peldin had always slouched toward. His face was young and unmarred by slumping, disease ravaged skin.

There was a lopsided grin under his worried brows, and I knew his expression so well.

"Ghost!" I cried, throwing myself into his solid arms.

He remained rigid for a moment.

"Peldin," I corrected myself, and he softened into the

embrace, squeezing me tightly in return.

"You did it. You saved me, Zari," he whispered into my hair.

My heart raced at the implications. Who was this man now? Would he be the sweet, playful ghost, or the sour but kind man? Maybe a combination of both. The idea of that made me smile.

I let go of him, suddenly bashful. "How do you feel?"

"Whole again. I remember everything now. I'm sorry to have scared you at the end there. I wasn't … myself." He glanced in the direction of his rooms then back to me, a crease cutting between his brows. "Thank you. I don't know how you did it."

"I found the person Darian forced to curse you, to take your magic." I rushed my words out, as though their speed could keep them ahead of the emotion chasing their heels. "It was my mother. I thought she'd left us, but she's been here, Darian's prisoner, the whole time."

The look of concern from Peldin sent a wash of heat through me as he moved closer. I was still frozen to the floor. He stopped inches from me, his icy-blue eyes looking down into mine, capturing my attention. "We'll work this out. We'll save her; don't worry. Now I know who I am, now I have my powers back, things are going to be different."

I shook my head, trying to clear the effects of his hypnotic gaze. I wanted to believe him. I knew he was powerful. But so was Darian. "We should hide. We can't let Darian know you're back. What if he curses you again and gets rid of me so I can't remind you who you are?"

Peldin smiled softly, a twinkle in his eye. He reached out and took my hand, leading me down the hall to where it opened up at the end to a small seating area near a window. He sat on one side of a small lounge and directed me to the other end.

Once I was seated, he said, "I've already made arrangements there. I've had some practice with the security system already, so we don't have to worry about any cameras or record of what you've been up to."

"When?"

"Right before I came to find you." He leaned back, propping his elbow on the back of the loveseat, resting his cheek against his hand. "We have all the time in the world."

"We don't." My anxiety still burbled. "Darian is going to come for us in the morning, to see that the task he set me is done."

The smile slipped from his face while his eyes hardened. Yup, there was the Peldin I remembered. "My brother is still untouchable. Even my magic can't break the protection spell he makes the ritualists cast on him every morning, and the only way to stop that spell would be to put their lives at risk, which I won't do."

My heart grew a size, warming away the anxiety.

"While the protection spell is in place, no matter how powerful I am, anything I do will only return on me three-fold." He turned his face away from me while dragging his fingers through his hair. When he turned back, his eyes were bright and intense. "Run with me. We can escape through that gap in the barrier. We'll take you mother, sister, father—whoever you want with us. Once we're out of Darian's reach, we can be free."

"I can't."

He started to protest, but I put a hand up to let him know I wasn't finished. "I mean, I *won't*. I won't run away without trying to stop Darian first. Not if it means leaving a single spellborn behind. Darian will continue to terrorize and enslave them even if we escape. I wouldn't be able to live with myself knowing I didn't stop him when I had the chance."

He raised an eyebrow at me. "I thought people didn't do things for others out of the kindness of their hearts?"

I rolled my eyes. "Okay, so I'm jaded, but I know when I'm wrong. Some people don't but there are many who will. And I want to be one of them. I want to be like you. Are you happy now I've admitted it?"

"Just a little." A long silence fell between us, and I couldn't stop staring at the healthy glow of Peldin's face. The playful grin there rekindled a deeper hope. That we wouldn't just

take Darian down, but that we could survive doing so. That we could go on together, and explore whatever these feelings between us were. I wanted to know if this care, this warmth, and connection I felt for Peldin could become something more, and whether he felt the same way.

Warmth brushed my cheek as Peldin's finger wiped away the tear I hadn't realized was there. It was strange to feel him as solid and tangible. "Zari, you surprise and impress me constantly. Whatever you're planning to do, I'm with you. I'll do everything I can to keep you safe."

"I know," I whispered.

I still had the plan that had come to me when I'd decided to turn back from my escape the first time. With Peldin by my side, I had more hope than ever that it could succeed.

"I need to talk to Rahanna. We're going to need her help."

TWENTY-TWO

MY ENTIRE BODY was a bundle of nerves. After making arrangements with Rahanna, I tried to get a couple of hours sleep before the riskiest part of my plan was put into action. I drifted fitfully, my head full of nightmares in which I had gotten Ghost's identity wrong. And when I told him he was Peldin, he'd morph into a gruesome version of Darian who cast a spell that stole his brother from existence. After that, it had gotten worse as Darian ran rampant through Oramont, a massive, unstoppable, magical titan.

I was a wreck when it came to the most crucial moment of my plan, but now I had Peldin and his magic on my side it was much easier than it would have been alone. I managed to hold it together. I managed to pull it off. And Darian had no idea.

Afterwards, I met Peldin back in his room with but an hour to spare in the twenty-four limit. I pulled back the ritualist's hood from my head and exhaled loudly. "It's done."

Peldin stood to greet me, and I was awed at the health and strength that had returned to his body. He still leaned a little to the side, but as though it was more habit than a weakness.

"Ready to be you again?"

I nodded, and felt his magic wash over me. He examined my face, rubbing his thumb softly along my lower eyelid, probably as deep a purple as my fading bruises. "We still have a bit before your time is up. You could get a little more sleep."

I shook my head. "No, I want to go and end this now. Thanks for your help last night. I don't think this plan would have had a chance without you."

"We make a good team." Peldin gave me a smile full of confidence and pride, and held out his hand. I took it, and we walked together to the elevator.

"Is this really going to work?" I asked for the millionth time as I pushed the button with a shaking finger.

"I'll do everything I can to make sure it does. It's the only way I can guarantee you'll one day stand in your own gondola and sing to a modestly attractive man in a Venice canal."

It took me a moment to understand who he meant. Peldin felt much more than just modestly attractive to me. He was a man I had grown to care for in both his disease-ravaged body and his whisp-of-smoke ghost-like form. It was his kind soul that glowed with beauty.

He gave me the hope and strength to believe that maybe my dreams could come true.

I grinned cheekily at him as we stepped into the golden lift. "I'm pretty good with rhythm and learning songs, but I never did learn to sing very well. Someone is going to have to endure a lot of singing practice."

"Is that an offer? Because it sounds lovely to me." His gaze took my breath away and almost made me forget where we were.

The elevator dinged, and the doors opened.

Peldin whispered softly, "Ready to avenge all the spellborn Darian has hurt or would hurt in the future?"

"You bet I am."

Together, we strode right into Darian's office.

He turned from his bar. "Zari? What are—"

Then he saw Peldin beside me, whole and healthy.

Darian's face went from smug self-reassurance, to confusion, then outrage. His ever-present crystal glass of amber liquid slipped through his fingers and crashed on the ground, breaking into large shards.

"What did you do? You disobedient little street rat!" Darian hit a button on his desk before he walked around and leaned casually against it. The smug look reappeared on his

face. "I still have the destruction curse and plenty of ritualists who can cast it again. You've messed up real good this time. You can say goodbye to that little sister you love so much."

"Nothing is going to happen to Nia. You're finished, Darian." My words rang with a confidence I didn't know I had.

Darian let loose a demented chuckle. "You can't stop me. No one can touch me—not even a thaumaturgist. I always win. How do you not know this by now?"

The sound of the door opening and footsteps thundering in were ignored as I strode right up to Darian and smashed my fist into his nose.

A crack echoed through the silent room, as though everyone had frozen, everyone had held their breaths.

Pain erupted in my knuckles, but I shook it out easily.

It was Darian's smug confidence, Darian's nose that had cracked. It took a moment for the pain to register for him, as though it was so foreign, so inconceivable, he didn't even know what was happening.

"What … how?" Blood gushed from his nostrils, spilling over his white teeth, still bared in a faltering smile. His hands clutched at his nose.

Gasps and whispers erupted behind me. I glanced back to see a crowd of security and ritualists summoned by Darian. They all stared, unmoving and wary, not one of them stepping forward to help.

A CAGE OF GOLD AND LIES

Darian pulled his hands away from his face, revealing bright red skin and a crooked nose. "This is impossible! My protection spell was cast this morning as it always is."

"It sure was. You just didn't know who cast it."

Confusion warred with fury, and Darian spat, "I'm not stupid. I was there! The ritualist said the spell perfectly. They know what would happen if they don't."

I grinned. "I did say the spell perfectly. Shame I don't have a single bit of magic to actually make it work though."

I had convinced Rahanna to let me take her place casting the protection spell that morning. I'd learned the spell when I'd heard her perform it, and saw then too how little notice Darian took of his daily servants. My initial plan had been to take the chance that Darian wouldn't care which of his loyal ritualists stood there reciting the words from under their shadowy hood, as long as it was done. To simply hope he didn't notice it was me. It would have been a huge risk, but one I was willing to take. Once I'd saved Peldin though, my plan became much stronger. He charmed me to look and sound like Rahanna for the ritual. And Rahanna had confirmed that Darian would feel no physical difference from the spell being cast. He wouldn't know if it worked or didn't. Not until my fist met his face.

"You?" Darian spluttered. "But you're a *thaumaturgist*; you cast all those spells."

"Nope. I really did try to tell you, but you wouldn't believe me. Every test you set me, I passed with help from someone else," I turned to smile at Peldin over my shoulder.

"Then you'll all be punished!" Darian roared. He waved his arms at the ritualists and security surrounding us. "Kill her! Kill them both!" He pointed a finger at me and his brother, his face bright red and a vein jutting out on his forehead.

"No!" Cam stepped forward in front of the others. "It's true. Zari really has no magic. Darian's protection spell is down. He's powerless. As long as none of us go to his aid, he can't control us anymore."

I nodded to him. "Right here, right now, we stand up for ourselves, and each other, against Darian King."

There were shuffles, murmurs. For a moment, I half expected some of them to rush Darian and beat him into person-jam, judging by the looks they gave him. Instead, they moved to stand beside Peldin and me, united.

Darian's voice was a strangled cry. "I'll have all your loved ones tortured and killed for betraying me."

"Can't betray someone you never felt loyalty for." I turned toward Darian, ready to tell him to stand down and admit he was beat.

His hand has inches from my neck, wielding a large shard of broken glass.

A CAGE OF GOLD AND LIES

Before I could move, someone brushed my shoulder, then Peldin was beside me.

Darian's hands crashed into an invisible wall. He reached back and pounded his fists on it, the one clasping the glass shard growing bloody. "No!" Taking several steps back, he stumbled and fell. "This can't be happening."

"Presenting the true thaumaturgist who has helped me all along," I announced to the rest of the room, waving my hand to Peldin. Awed whispers followed, along with shock as some recognized who he actually was.

He glared down at Darian, fury glittering in his gaze. "Now, with all my power, what shall I do with you, dear brother? Erase you from existence? Wouldn't that be fitting? Or maybe split your spirit from your body, leaving you roaming the halls as a ghost with no recollection of his past?"

"You can have it, have it back—the estate, every-thing. Have anything you want," Darian gibbered, pleading as he scooted away across the floor.

Peldin's eyes softened. "I find, after all you've put me through and all I've experienced recently, that I have somewhat simpler desires than I once did. I don't wish for revenge. I only wish for safety. Which means a world that your cruelty and manipulation cannot touch."

A bright gold light pierced the room.

It turned red and then faded to reveal Darian missing.

In his place was a red rose in mid-bloom.

I gaped. "Did you just change him into a rose?"

"I did." Peldin waved his hand again and the rose disappeared from the floor, and reformed in a glass display. He stepped closer to it, inspecting the magical bloom with a soft frown before turning back to me. "For now, at least. We can decide his final fate later. There is so much more we have to do first. Undoing the harm he caused will be a lot of work, but today is the start of a new King empire."

Together, we turned back to the spellborn gathered behind us. Cam had stepped forward, as though ready to protect me as well, and I gave him a warm smile. In the very back of the crowd I spotted Rahanna, hidden by her hood, wary disbelief in battle with hope in her gaze.

A range of emotions played across all their faces, as though worrying they had traded one cruel and powerful master for another.

I wasn't sure what I would say to comfort everyone, to explain. I had only thought through up to stopping Darian.

Peldin checked with a quick glance to me, and I nodded for him to take over.

"I am Peldin King. You probably don't recognize me this way. Zari helped restore me to my former health by breaking a curse Darian had forced onto me. And also thanks to her, as you can see, Darian's reign has ended. He can't hurt you

or your loved ones anymore. What Darian did to each and every one of you was wrong, and I'll do everything I can to make reparations. I only wish I had seen the darkness in my brother and stopped him before things got this bad." He turned briefly to look at the rose. "I'm sure you all have a lot of questions, and I will answer them later. Right now, just know that you are free."

The word sang, echoing through my heart. *Free.*

We'd done it.

An immense weight lifted from me. *I'm free.* Truly free. And I'd achieved that with the help of people I cared for, who also cared for me, and I was able to free them too.

The spellborn milled about, still unsure. Some whispered; some hugged each other. Others cried tears of joy.

A huge grin cracked my face. "Go on. Go and spread the news!"

They moved quickly, dashing off in different directions, some gleefully using their magic to vanish in a flash of light.

Rahanna ran over and wrapped her arms around me as she gave me a tight hug. "Thank you," she whispered. I returned her hug, confident I'd soon be seeing more of the person she used to be.

"I couldn't have done it without you. Thank you for your bravery this morning." It had been hard for her to take the risk of swapping roles for those brief moments. But she'd

chosen hope, and trust, and helped make this happen.

She nodded to me, tears streaming over cheeks puffed up by her smile, then she spoke a spell and vanished in a flash of light.

Soon, Peldin and I were alone.

He looked at the rose again, and I wondered what memories and regrets must be filling his head.

I moved next to him and rested my shoulder on his. "Why a rose?"

"Because they are beautiful, and if you're not careful, they can hurt you. And it was either that or a toad, and I was worried people might neglect looking after the toad." Peldin gave me one of his playful grins and turned to me. He ran his finger down my cheek to where some of the worst bruises still marred my jawline. "Now, we don't need these anymore, do we?"

Peldin didn't wait for me to answer. Within seconds, the low ache throughout my face that I had gotten so used to was gone. Its absence felt like freedom. I touched my fingertips to my cheeks, prodding gently without pain.

He really was a miracle worker. His power awed me.

Peldin strode in a small circle around the grand room, glancing out the window that showed Oramont beyond, running a finger over the expensive desk. "I wasn't entirely truthful when I said the only thing I wanted was safety." He finished back in front of me. He ducked his head as though embarrassed. "There's one more thing I desire. And it's you. I would give up all of this and be the happiest man alive to live a small and comfortable life with you by my side. If you also want that too."

My lower lip trembled as emotions rushed through me. I did want that.

Peldin's playfulness was infectious though, and I looked skeptically at him. "As long as it's a life where we can still go to Venice."

He barked a laugh. "Of course. We could give up ninety-nine-point-nine-nine-nine et cetera percent of this misgotten wealth and still live rich lives."

I liked how he used *we*. But the thought of being in a relationship brought out a small, scared part of me. I grew more serious again. "I still have a lot to work out about who I am. I've never had a relationship beyond being responsible for my family. I do want to be with you, spend time with you, but I …" How could I tell him I was worried that a new relationship might feel like as much of a cage as my past responsibilities?

"I understand. We can take things as slow as needed. I can wait for you." Peldin's voice was so earnest it seemed to reach out and squeeze my heart. "Your freedom is something I will never, ever take from you."

I covered my face with both hands, stifling a sob. How could he be so perfectly kind?

"Thank you," I murmured through the gaps between my fingers.

"Now, are you ready to free your mother, then go and surprise your sister?"

My hands dropped away and I nodded fervently.

"Come on. We have one more thing we have to do on the way." Peldin stuck his hand out and I grasped it. We took a step forward, and in a flash of light, we appeared on the paved drive right by the front gates.

Gossip had spread and spellborn were already gathering in the grounds nearby, seeking their promised exit.

Peldin flung his free hand into the sky. The perimeter spell lit up in a bright blue color, then bursts of red crackled through it. A giant *snap* sent a blast of air into my face as the barrier shattered and the pieces flew into the air. Before I could ask what was happening, the shards burst into bright flashing fireworks. Every color I could imagine lit up the sky as he destroyed the magical wall that had been used to imprison the spellborn.

He gave me a lopsided grin. "Probably a bit too flashy, but it seemed appropriate for the occasion."

"It's beautiful."

Everyone watched the fireworks as they cheered and

hugged each other. Then most of them disappeared, hopefully returning to their families.

I looked up at Peldin, the fireworks reflecting brightly over his ice-blue irises. "Seeing all this wonderful magic going on, I'm kind of feeling jealous all of a sudden."

Peldin looked deeply into my eyes. "Zari, you're the most magical thing I've ever seen."

TWENTY-THREE

I NEVER DID come into magic.

Ma had it and Nia turned out to be a powerful ritualist too, but it had entirely skipped me.

I didn't mind so much.

I'd learned I could make my own kind of magic, with bravery, kindness, and love.

"If you don't stop working, we'll be late to the party."

I looked up from the stack of papers I'd been reading through to see Peldin leaning over our large shared desk.

"I know. I just really want to pass this exam." I placed the printouts down on top of my economics textbook. One of the first things I'd decided to do once free again was finish high school, and I was deep in the final tests for my online course.

What I was learning had proven to be useful in my new life at the Crystal Estate. After we'd released the spellborn, Peldin had gone to work right away in restructuring the estate and the King family businesses. He called on me as a consultant often, knowing that his life experience didn't give him the right perspective to understand what it was like for most people in the workforce.

His first suggestions revolved around higher pay and proper breaks. But I'd pushed for more. When I explained what I wanted, he'd agreed happily. Back when he'd told me he'd give up all his wealth, I hadn't truly believed him, but he proved himself when he followed my suggestion and created company co-op structures for all of the King businesses, which put the ownership and profits of each business into the hands of those who worked there.

And he started with the cotton-processing plant where I used to work. I was at the handover ceremony and got to see the smiles of complete shock from Vera and the others as they realized they now owned shares in their own business. It was wonderful.

"You know it all already. You've got this. You deserve a night off," Peldin said. Then he leaned in and winked. "And if you don't pass, maybe your boyfriend can just magically fix things up for you."

I laughed, knowing his sense of humor by now, and also

knowing he'd never overstep in that way. Over the time we'd spent together in freedom, he'd proven that.

After Darian was gone, Peldin had invited me to stay on the estate, but at first, I wasn't comfortable being there, and I'd doubted Ma would be either. So we ended up in an apartment down in Oramont. Peldin helped with the whole process and never argued once, never tried to keep me by his side.

My family was whole again, and Peldin visited every day, calling in advance and asking for my opinions on everything, from how I thought he could push the city into better immigration laws, to where he should donate his old wheelchair. He kept things casual, taking me for coffee, or letting me take him to try manakish. We grew so much together during that time, and my feelings for him had grown stronger as well.

After a while, he invited me back to the estate for lunch. It was strange setting foot there again. He took me on a walk, saying he wanted to discuss something important, but wouldn't tell me what. He led me over to the tree house he'd played with Darian in as a kid—the place where I had decided not to run, but to face my life and fight for freedom.

I should have known right then he was up to something. He'd climbed up a few rungs, then turned around, holding his hand out for me. Inside, he'd laid out a soft blanket. I could still remember the plush feel under me as I sat beside him there. I disappeared into the memory, reliving it.

He sat in front of me, folding his legs. "I want you to do me a favor."

I shrugged, finding myself staring at his lips as I had often lately. "Sure, depending on what it is."

"Close your eyes?" he asked.

"Oooookay?" I did, and sat waiting in the darkness.

Peldin's voice was close to me. "I want to take you somewhere. Are you ready to go with me?"

"Yes." The answer popped out, full of curiosity, trust, and without hesitation.

It hadn't felt like very long when he spoke again. "Okay, open your eyes."

The first thing I saw was Peldin watching my face intently.

Then I realized we weren't in the tree house anymore. I was sitting on a gondola seat, with him opposite me.

"No way!" I gasped.

The boat had intricate carvings on the bow with colorful highlights, and a small flag standing proud. We bobbed softly in the water, and I looked right around me, taking in the view.

Peldin chuckled. "Just so you know, your expression right now is priceless."

"I don't even care. This is awesome!" I shuffled over the bright blue cushions and rug and looked over the edge of

the boat. The teal water of the canal contrasted against the yellow bricks of the building we sailed past. I reached a hand down, letting the water slide by my fingers. Little pieces of the architecture stood out as we went under a bridge. Time flew by as we went through the canals. Peldin's hand found mine and we enjoyed the ride together.

Soon, I had soaked in enough of the view of Venice and turned to look at Peldin instead, taking in the curves of his smile that I loved so much. That was when I knew. That was when I leaned across the small bench and kissed him for the first time.

"Zari?" Peldin's voice in the present snapped me from the memory.

"I'm sorry, what?" I shook my head and looked around. Back in our office. One we shared at the estate, since I had moved back here. Peldin and I now had our own adjoining suites. It was nice living with him, and even nicer knowing Nia and my family were okay without me there to look after them.

"Tonight's important. I mean, your family will miss you if we don't make it to the party soon."

I smiled at him. "Okay, let's go have some fun."

Peldin held the door open for me as we made our way to the main courtyard. String lights made the area sparkle, and picnic rugs were spread everywhere, one for each spellborn family in attendance. There was no waitstaff, no entertainment.

It was a potluck, and as I walked through the patchwork of picnics under the starry sky, my heart soared to see everyone joyously sharing their food, and stories, and magic.

I saw Ma, and rushed over and gave her a big hug. I'd seen her every day since Peldin and I had freed her from Darian's prison, but I still gave her a hug every time like it was the moment I had freed her from her cell.

Nia jumped in on the hug too.

Sergio stayed off to one side, clearly not wanting to intrude. But I tilted my head to him and he joined the embrace too. Our reunion had been rough, but we were working on rebuilding our relationship. We'd managed to get him straight into a rehab, and into therapy for his PTSD and depression—something I could never have afforded in the past. The money all came from my and Ma's wages and compensation package. The same package that went out to all the spellborn who had been stolen by Darian.

Beyond that, Peldin had done something truly selfless. The Crystal Estate—this place, created from the magic and wealth of spellborns—was now owned by those spellborns. Peldin had given up his family home for them, now owning only a small portion himself, along with the portion I owned. Some spellborn sold off their shares immediately and left to live their lives elsewhere. But many stayed, like Cam, still eager to learn from those like him, and the change in the place was incredible. It was turning into a true community and school for those with magic.

For a while we mingled, checking in on how everyone was adjusting to the new normal. Nia practiced her magic with Ma and Cam, and I almost got bowled over by the sisters from the conjurer dorms I had covered for. And not only them. I received so many grateful hugs from people that I soon had to go for some alone time in a quiet part of the garden before I became a blubbering mess.

"I've been looking for you," Peldin said, appearing beside me.

"Sorry, I'll go back in a minute. Just needed a breather."

Peldin smiled, and looked around at the weeping willow overhead, the blue star flowers at our feet, and the full moon shining down. "No, actually, this is perfect."

"Huh?"

"I had thought about doing a grand display in front of everyone. But I think you'll like this better."

Peldin reached into his pocket, and then dropped onto one knee.

My breath clogged in my throat.

Peldin looked up at me with the ice-blue eyes I didn't know if I could live without. He clipped open a small box, presenting it to me. Inside sat a plain gold band.

"Zari, how we met was like something from a fairy tale.

It was dark and at times terrible, but together, we survived. Now I want our fairy tale to find its happily ever after. Will you do me the honor of marrying me?"

Time slowed as I took in Peldin's words. Tears welled in my eyes. "Yes!"

Peldin grabbed the ring and slipped it on my finger. I tried to pull him to his feet so I could hug him, but he didn't budge. Instead, he pointed to my hand. I looked at my ring and gasped as the gold band grew out with little leaves built into the metal. Emeralds appeared above the leaves, sparkling and vibrant. Sky-blue stones circled a large diamond that formed as the metal anchored it in place. The entire process was breathtaking.

"Show off," I laughed.

"All I did was enchant it to express the beauty of the wearer." As the ring finished, Peldin stood up and enveloped me in an embrace that lifted me from the ground.

He let me back down onto my feet and smiled. The man could move mountains with a flash of that smile … literally and figuratively. "I wasn't sure you'd say yes since we haven't discussed it, but I couldn't wait any longer." His hands cupped my face as he pressed a quick kiss to my lips. "I love you so much."

"It was a surprise, but I love it. I love you." I narrowed my eyes cheekily. "Maybe I should have expected this though.

You did once ask for my firstborn child.”

We laughed together, then our lips met again in a longer kiss, one full of passion and need.

“Just one firework?” Peldin whispered through his kiss.

“Okay.” I giggled back.

It exploded over us, but I didn’t look up, too deep in the kiss and my love for him.

THE END

ABOUT THE AUTHOR

WHETHER IT'S PAINTING artworks or writing novels, creating fantasy works is Selina's biggest passion. She lives in Australia with her husband and daughter and loves food, gardening, geekery, and all things fantasy.

FIND OUT MORE ABOUT SELINA

Official Website www.selinafenech.com

Memory's Wake Trilogy

A modern girl lost in and hunted in a fairy tale world. An illustrated young adult portal fantasy with Arthurian and Victorian themes.

Empath Chronicles

Teenagers with superpowers fueled by emotions … what could go wrong? A young adult superhero romance.

More Books by Selina A Fenech

Beshadowed

You have been lied to. Werewolves, vampires, ghosts … they aren't what you think. What is really lurking in the dark? A spooky urban fantasy.

Heartsblood

Her blood is irresistible, but is it worth the cost? A vampire romance for adults.